I0572083

VIPER

WAR BROTHERS MC

BIANCA LEE WARD

This book contains adult themes and is not suitable for persons under the age of 18.

For information regarding possible triggers, please see www.biancaleeward.com or contact info@biancaleeward.com.

Viper

ALSO BY BIANCA LEE WARD

AXLE

Book 0.5, War Brothers MC

She's the one woman I shouldn't want.
But I'll do anything to have her...

By popular demand, **Axle and Elena's** story is coming soon.
Pre-order is $0.99.

REAPER

Book 1, War Brothers MC

I let her go once because she wasn't mine.
This time, I'll die before I give her up…

I want her.

That smile… those curves.

But Ava doesn't belong to me.

Then she arrives in my clubhouse, seeking refuge. My gut churns at
the sight of the bruises on her face, the fear in her eyes.

Before I was the president of the War Brothers Motorcycle Club, I
was a special forces sniper who hunted down evil men like her

husband. Now I avoid relationships because the wounds I have are more than skin deep.

But Ava's different, and when I find her in the wrong bedroom—my bedroom—one night, what happens next changes everything.

I let her go once because she was married, but I won't make the same mistake twice.

I'll die before I let her dangerous husband, the jealous women in our club, or the enemy our club didn't see coming lay a finger on her.

Because this time around, Ava is mine.

Grab your copy of Reaper now.

**Bonus chapter for Reaper is coming in 2024,

only accessible if you're on my mailing list**

BOMBER

Book 2, War Brothers MC

I won't lose her again.

But our family secrets could tear us apart…

It's been ten years since I was forced to let Zara go. I joined the military and fought hard to forget her, but since I returned home to become our club's Sergeant at Arms, I've always watched from afar to make sure she's safe.

Now Zara is back in Crown Village on the anniversary of a traumatic event that changed her family forever. And I can't stay away.

I can see the longing for me in her eyes, yet she hesitates to get too close. She's scared to trust me again, and I don't blame her.

When new information linked to her family tragedy comes to light, I'm determined to help solve the mystery and find the answers she needs because the War Brothers MC protects our own.

But digging up the past means revealing secrets that someone wants to remain dead and buried. And when they're uncovered, they have the power to destroy our bond forever…

Grab your copy of Bomber now.

**Bonus chapter of Bomber is coming in 2024,

only accessible if you're on my mailing list**

Get ready for **more** stories in 2025!

Sign up for my mailing list to be the first to hear all about it.

PLAYLIST

Figured You Out – Nickelback
Something Really Bad– Dizzee Rascal feat. Will.I.Am
You Make Me Feel – Cobra Starship feat. Sabi
In The Dark – Dev
Hangover – Taio Cruz feat. Flo Rida
Falling – Stafford Brothers feat. Ollie James
I Want You To Know – Zedd feat. Selena Gomez
LoveGame – Lady Gaga
Night & Day – Silver Sneakerz
Flaunt It – TV Rock
Smile – Avril Lavigne
Little Bad Girl – David Guetta feat. Taio Cruz & Ludacris
Delirious – Steve Aoki, Chris Lake, Tujamo feat. Kid Ink
Work Bitch – Britney Spears
Only Girl (In The World) - Rihanna
Take Over Control – Afrojack
Shape Of You (Rock Version) – Our Last Night
Sucker – Our Last Night
Hello – Stafford Brothers feat. Lil Wayne & Christina Milian
Good For You – Selena Gomez feat. A$AP Rocky
Blank Space – I Prevail
Feel Something – Illenium, Excision & I Prevail
She Likes/Blvck/Slayer – Bryce Savage
Little Girl Gone – Chinchilla
Sexy Bitch – David Guetta feat. Akon
American Horror Show – Snow Wife
Can You Feel My Heart – Bring Me To The Horizon
Just Pretend – Bad Omens

DEDICATION

To the extroverted women with hearts of gold—never change.

ONE
PARTY EXCITEMENT

Sophie

Ping!

I pick up my phone from the bar to see a new message from Sexy Cop with Nice Teeth. When I open the message, I see the ugliest dick pic I have ever seen. My head falls back as laughter erupts from my mouth. The dick is thick but short and slightly discolored, like there's something wrong with the skin, nestled in dense pubic hair, which only makes it appear smaller.

My brother Lawson's brows curve in as he squints at me. "What's so funny?" he asks as the barman pours his whiskey, so I turn my phone around and shove it in his face. The disgusted grunt that comes from his mouth makes me laugh again. He pushes my phone away. "Get that deformed dick away from me."

This is the phone I use when I want some dick. It's where all the men's numbers go. I enlarge the photo and bring it closer to my face to inspect it. "The skin is all weird, like he needs to drink more water or something."

I peek up at Lawson. His glass is at his mouth and he's taking a sip, his critical eyes still on me. A spark of awareness hits me, and I grin. "It looks like a yam!"

My brother chokes. He hisses and sets his glass back down on the counter as he wipes dribbles of whiskey off his chin.

I press on the image and forward it in a message to my best friend, Piper. I tap my fingers on the counter, waiting for her reply. I know Piper's read it when her name pops up on my screen, calling me.

I can't even say hi because she opens with, "What the actual fuck is that?"

I giggle. "If I had to see it, so did you! Don't you think it looks like a yam?"

She squeals. "It does. You're so right. I'll never be able to look at a yam the same."

"It's up there with the ugliest dicks I've ever seen," I say as I've seen plenty.

Piper and I both have active sex lives. We love sex, and we aren't ashamed of it. Some people have rosters of people they sleep with—we have waitlists.

"Do you remember a year ago, I told you about the guy who licked pussy like a champ, but his dick resembled a mushroom?" asks Piper.

I suck in a breath through my teeth, my hand coming to my mouth. "Yes! How could I forget?" Piper called me up at 2 a.m., drunk, telling me how she got pounded by a mushroom, so I ended up calling her Mario for a month. "What happened to that guy, anyway?"

She sighs. "Good times. I don't talk to him, so I wouldn't know. Who does the yam belong to?"

"Remember I told you about a hot cop who pulled over the limousine up in Crown Village and gave the driver a warning for speeding, and the cop and I exchanged numbers?"

"Faintly."

"Yes, it's him… such a shame. I don't understand what they expect me to say when they send me a dick pic. Like, oh yeah… I can't wait to suck on that."

She laughs. "It's because they're incapable of having a conversation with the opposite sex. They think they're going to make your panties damp by sending a dick pic, and that man didn't even make an effort. The lighting is poor, and there's a pile of dirty clothes in the background. What a turnoff!"

"I agree… dick pics are just wrong!"

"Sophie!" my brother whines. "Stop talking about it."

"Which brother is that?" Piper asks.

I raise my brow. She's met all three of my brothers a handful of times, and she seems to have a little crush on one of them.

"It's Lawson, not Alec."

"I have no idea what you're talking about," she says coyly, with a hint of amusement in her tone.

"Well… I better get going. I've got lunch with Dad, then I've got to get ready for tonight."

"I bet you're excited for lunch."

"Ha-ha," I deadpan.

"What are you getting ready for? Oh, wait… is that the combined bachelor and bachelorette party for your cousin Knox and his fiancée?"

A thrill of excitement courses through me. "It sure is for Knox and his partner, Zara."

"Isn't he in a motorcycle club?"

I do a little dance on my stool. "Uh-huh! They call themselves the War Brothers MC, and they're all going to be at the party tonight. I'm keen to get laid by a man in leather."

"Damn it, Sophie!" my brother pipes up again, but I ignore him.

"You lucky bitch! Have you seen what they look like?" asks Piper.

"I got a peek a couple of times, and they are fine as hell."

She lets out a gush of air. "I'm so jealous. Have fun. But before you go, when are you coming back to New York? Do you know how much longer you'll be staying in Crown Village?"

I've been back and forth between Crown Village and New York since Zara's sister Misty's vigil. Misty disappeared for ten years, so Zara's family held a vigil to remind the community of Misty vanishing. When the truth about Misty's disappearance was unveiled, the facts of the case affected Zara's and Knox's families and had knock-on effects on everyone, including my family. "I don't know how long I'll be here," I reply. I grew up with Zara and Knox, so I've been trying to show my support to everyone in Crown Village where I can.

"I'll have to get you to visit," I tell her. "You'll love it here." I've been staying at our family's five-star luxury resort. My father's and Alec's offices, from which they manage our Crown businesses, are also there. I've had no recent modeling shows, and since I returned to Crown Village, I've been working from my laptop and phone, managing my club business with the manager I've employed.

"I'd love to visit," Piper mumbles.

"I miss your face!" I say. "Bye! Love you."

"Love you too," she replies.

Lawson and I are at the bar at our resort, which is quite busy considering it's not even noon yet.

"You know you don't have to keep coming back here," Lawson says.

"I know," but I've been trying to be present during this difficult time. "Have you helped with Zara's charity?" I ask

Lawson. Zara created a charity to help women and children in the community to honor her sister, Misty.

"I've offered to help, but it seems they have more than enough people. I think I'm going to donate money. What about you?"

I give him a sharp nod. "Good idea. I'll do the same."

I get up to leave. I peer down at the time on my phone. "I'd better get going. I'm meeting Dad for lunch. See you tonight. What time do we have to be ready by?" I ask.

"Alec arranged for the jet to depart at six, arriving in Vegas at seven."

The barman pours another drink for Lawson. When I see the Crown Whiskey label, I smile. Lawson runs our Crown Village whiskey distillery. He has projected the business and receives orders from around the world.

After exiting the bar, I make my way to the Crown restaurant. Luxury and wealth drip off every inch of this building. The restaurant offers fine dining in an intimate setting, with striking lighting and large windows. It's famous for its fresh produce, innovative menu, and views of the beach. No sneakers, jeans, or sweatshirts allowed.

The woman behind the podium grins broadly at me. "Sophie, your table is reserved by the window."

The waiter next to her puts an arm out. "This way."

"I can make my way over, thank you. Can I please have a glass of sparkling water?"

The waiter bobs his head. "I'll get that for you right away, ma'am."

The staff are professional. Dad ensures he hires the best. I guess it's where I learned that hiring great staff is one component of building a successful business.

I give the waiter a small smile, walk over to the two-seater by the window, and take a seat in the plush chairs. The waiter swiftly returns with a bottle of sparkling water and pours it into the glass for me.

"Thank you." As I take a sip, the waiter gasps from beside me, and the restaurant quietens.

"Where's my daughter?" Dad's loud voice echoes. There's an undercurrent of unease in the air as I place my glass on the table and glance up to see my father striding toward me.

He's the most distinguished man in the room, and it has nothing to do with his good looks or the expensive suits he wears. His presence alone exudes confidence and authority. Glancing at the other patrons, I notice all eyes on him. Tall, with gray-and-black peppered hair, strong features, and broad shoulders, he commands attention. The waiter stands up straighter beside me.

I stand and smile as my father reaches our table. We share a brief hug, and I kiss him on the cheek. "Hello, Dad."

He gives me a sharp nod. "Sophie, how has your morning been?"

I think back to the dick pic and barely hold back a laugh. "Quite amusing. How has your day been?"

He opens his mouth to answer, but his eyes narrow, locking onto a small crease in the linen. Dad's gaze cuts to the waiter. "There's a crease," he points out as his fingers trail over it. "All linen must be wrinkle-free," he spits acid, making me cringe. I bite my tongue. I don't agree with how he speaks to people, but he's the only parent I have left, so I try not to cause conflict.

I can sense others' curious stares. Even though I should be used to Dad's criticism, I still feel bad for the waiter, who has paled. "I'm so sorry," the waiter stutters.

Elizabeth, the manager, rushes to our table. "Is everything okay, Mr. Crown?" she asks, her voice dripping with panic and concern.

He points to the crease in the linen. "If I am not receiving impeccable table settings, I can only imagine what other customers are receiving. Our guests expect a fine dining experience. Pay attention to *every* detail."

"It won't happen again." She peers at the waiter. "Ambroise, I will be Mr. Crown and Sophie's server today." The waiter bobs his head in acknowledgment and darts away.

Elizabeth gracefully unfolds our linen napkins and places them in our laps. Dad watches her like a hawk, most likely to make sure the table service is perfect.

Dad's eyes return to me. "I've been very busy with work."

I nod because I try to stay out of our family's businesses. That has never interested me. Dad's smart, a workaholic, and cold-hearted—the perfect businessman—though I think he thaws the tiniest bit when he's with me. Maybe because I'm his only daughter.

We order lunch and keep our conversation to a minimum. He answers his phone throughout our meal, making me wonder why he organized lunch to begin with.

I TWIRL IN FRONT OF THE LONG WARDROBE MIRROR AND WATCH AS the long red dress flutters around me, showcasing my leg that's poking out of the thigh-high split. The dress has a fitted halter neck and a flowing skirt. I grasp the glass and throw back the shot of whiskey, then walk into the kitchen and put the glass in the sink.

When I get to the front door, I slide my feet into my Christian Louboutins and sling my gold Gucci purse over my shoulder. Giddiness sparks through my body. I take one last peek in the mirror by the front door, checking my red lipstick, before I make my way to the limousine waiting in the parking bay in front of the resort.

When I open the door, Alec and Lawson are already inside, though I'm not surprised. I give them a small smile as I shuffle along the seat facing them.

"We are going to a nightclub, Alec. At least take the tie off. It looks like you've come from the office." He's wearing a damn suit to a social get-together. He adjusts his tie, which is already straight. Lawson is a bit more appropriately dressed in a blue collared shirt and dark blue jeans. "Have you heard from Harrison?" I ask them.

"He's late… as per usual," answers Alec.

Sometimes I wonder how my parents gave birth to both Alec and Harrison. They are opposites. There's Mr. I-Have-a-Pole-Stuck-up-My-Ass and Mr. Casual, who is the courageous firefighter. Harrison is easygoing and gives no fucks about being a part of the family business… just like me.

I pull my phone from my clutch and message Piper.

Piper

One hour to Vegas woohooo!

I'm so jealous. Have a great time with the sexy bikers and don't do anything I wouldn't do *wink*

Fifteen minutes later, the door opens, and Harrison slides in next to me. "Sorry I'm late."

Alec grunts in response.

"Love the dress, sis."

I smile back at Harrison. "Thank you." He's wearing a fitted white shirt, black jeans, and white sneakers. "Very handsome. You're going to fit right in with the MC. Have you met any of them?"

He smiles. "Only occasionally around town. They mainly stick to themselves, so I don't know much about them. Knox, or should I say Bomber, since that's his MC name, is close with two he served with in the military, Reaper and Viper."

I quirk a brow. "Are they single?"

"Reaper has a partner, but I think Viper is single."

"What's Viper look like?"

"Uh… six foot, dark-blond hair. When I've seen him, he's always smiling, and I've heard he's smooth with the ladies."

I smile, excited to meet him.

AFTER LANDING IN OUR PRIVATE JET, WE'RE PICKED UP BY A limousine and are on our way. A phone pings with a message. Alec's phone lights up. He has been liaising with Knox about what we're doing tonight.

"What time's the jet picking us up after the party?" I ask Alec.

"I haven't organized a time," he replies.

I smirk. "That's unlike you."

He raises a brow. "I didn't know what *your* and *Harrison's* plans were."

Harrison chuckles from beside me. "Good, because I plan on having a big night."

"So do I."

TWO
FORMING A PLAN TO MAKE HER MINE

Viper

"SHOTS! SHOTS! SHOTS!" AXLE, MY MC BROTHER, HOLLERS AS he walks toward us with a tray of shots.

I rub my hands together. "Fuck yeah!" I reply enthusiastically. My mission is celebrating Bomber and Zara's soon-to-be marriage, but I also want to sleep with Bomber's cousin Sophie. I don't want to get too drunk because if I can get her in the sheets, I want to remember every curve of her body, her taste, her scent—everything about her. I'm aware I'll be lucky to ever sleep with someone as classy as her again.

I've caught a glimpse of Sophie a few times, while she's been back. If it were a different woman, I would have at least chatted her up. I shake my head. Well… tonight's my chance.

When I pick up the overfilled shot glass, the liquid trickles down and onto my hand. I wait until everyone has a shot in their hand, and then I raise mine. "To Bomber and Zara," I yell.

Everyone cheers, "To Bomber and Zara."

We clink our shot glasses together, then I toss the shot down my throat, feeling the burn. I'm left with a sweet taste in my mouth, but I enjoy it better than the last shot.

"What's the name of that one?" I ask Axle, having to raise my voice over the music.

His grin widens. "Wet pusssyyyyyy," he replies, making me laugh.

"No wonder I like the taste of it then," I say with a wink, then turn my attention to Ava. "Aren't you having any shots tonight?" She hasn't touched one that's been brought out.

Her eyes widen, but then she smiles. "No, thank you. I'm happy with my cocktail."

My brows lift. I bet it's a mocktail. I peer at her, then Reaper, her partner and the president of the MC. He subtly shakes his head at me, as in telling me to leave the topic. How stupid do they think I am? She's pregnant. I have no doubt about it. I'm patiently waiting for them to tell everyone.

Alec did an awesome job organizing Bomber and Zara's party. We got VIP access to this exclusive nightclub called Envy, so we didn't have to line up, and he got us a VIP table. But the best part is Alec set up a tab, so we don't have to pay for a drink all night.

The second floor is classier. Everything from the furniture to the lighting to the VIP bar. I settle back in my seat. I'm stoked that the sweet butts didn't come. Candy is a cool chick and all… but she's getting way too clingy. We have sex, that's it. I'm not interested in anything more. Having casual sex with her is convenient. I've told her time and time again what the deal is between us.

I lean over, putting my empty glass on the table. I peer around at the couples surrounding me. It feels like everyone is settling down. Axle and Elena, Reaper and Ava, now Bomber and Zara. The men will be attached to the women's hips tonight, never allowing them to go too far away. Possessive psychos. Though I don't blame them—I'd trust no man outside the club.

There's a twinge of jealousy I haven't experienced before. Seeing all the couples together and how well everyone gets along has me wondering if I want more than just hookups. I clear my throat... I can't believe that crossed my mind. Bomber and Zara's engagement and their promise of a happily ever after is messing with my head.

There's me, Twitch, Demon, Cash, and Rage, the last men standing, though I'm sure someone will be next. Twitch might sleep with Mercedez, one of the MC's sweet butts, but he's not interested in a relationship with her. And as much as he pines over Reaper's sister, Milly, he's got no chance. Rage is in his early twenties, still too young for anything serious, and I could laugh at Demon ever getting a woman. Perhaps it will be Cash, but according to the men, he still hasn't moved on from his past relationship.

I walk by our table and to the balcony that leads over to the first floor. The lights are dim where we are, with different colored flashing lights coming from the main stage. My shoulders move to the beat of techno music. Steve Aoki is killing it tonight. The first level is packed with people dancing.

There's a squeal, so I turn to see Zara standing, hugging Sophie. Harrison, Alec, and Lawson are off to the side, shaking hands with the MC men. Their family is beyond wealthy—like generational, old-money wealthy. Sophie looks incredible in a red dress that shows off her long legs. As I turn my gaze to the side to get a better sight of her, the slit in her dress reveals the creamy skin of her thigh. She should model for Victoria's Secret because she's an absolute bombshell.

I lean back on the edge of the balcony, drinking her in. I first saw her at Zara's sister's vigil, and I've never been so taken by a woman. I couldn't even go and talk to her, so I sussed her out, asking Zara and Bomber to give me the lowdown. Sophie used to be close to them when they were young, but they haven't kept in touch since she finished school, then moved away to New York.

Sophie is devoted. Coming home when her family and friends need her. She had a career on a silver platter because of all the businesses her family owns but moved away instead to pursue her own dreams. Sophie isn't just a beauty, she seems to be so much more, and that has piqued my interest. I've never wanted to spend more than one wild night with a woman, but I want to get to know her.

That we do business with her father should be reason enough not to go there because it could cause problems, but right now I'm living in the present. I can worry about all the other nonsense later.

When the men have shaken Bomber's cousins' hands, I step forward. I grasp Alec's hand in a firm handshake. He's a nice guy and all, but he looks like a tool being in a club with a suit on… though maybe that's his game. Showing women that he's loaded, because the Crowns are the richest people I've ever met.

Lawson's next, and we shake hands. "Hey," I say to him. He's a sexy son of a bitch, I'll give him that. My eyes drift over the family. They all are a good-looking bunch.

I pull back on seeing Harrison. His smile is wide. "Hey, man, how are you doing?" I ask him. He always says hi to me even though we don't know him well. He's dressed in a casual shirt and jeans, like the rest of us.

"Awesome… now." He glances around the club. "I haven't been back to Vegas in so long."

"I haven't either. The clubs are insane," I reply. I'm used to the parties back home in the MC clubhouse or at our local bar.

Harrison looks around, then tilts his head. "I'm going to the bar; do you want anything?"

I nod. "A beer, thanks."

"What type?"

"Anything will do."

He nods, then makes his way over to the bar as Sophie walks over to me. My pulse thrums. I scold myself for acting like a pussy. I can't stop my eyes from wandering down her breasts to the curve of her hips to those long legs that I hope to be spreading tonight.

"Viper, is it?" she says, and I like the way my name rolls off her tongue a little too much. I'm getting a semi.

I inch back, giving her an indecent grin. "Sure is, darlin'."

I swear to God, I saw her mouth the word "delicious," but with the damn music up so loud, I can't hear shit. She pulls me in for a hug, which startles me for a second, but then I hug her back, appreciating her body against mine.

I take a deep breath and say, "You smell heavenly…" Mouth-watering and appetizing.

She leans back, giving me a seductive smile. "So do you… like coconut and lime."

Now I have a raging hard-on. She's giving me the eyes already, and I just met her. "Do you come to Vegas often?" I ask.

"No, but I'm in the clubbing scene," she says as she peers down at the crowd.

"It's a pretty good setup here," I say.

She arches a perfectly shaped brow. "Mine's better."

"Yours? What do you mean?"

She grins. "I own a club in New York."

I knew she left Crown Village for her modeling career, but I didn't know she owned a club. Beauty and brains. What a dangerous combination. "Businesswoman, hey… I'm impressed." She gives me a funny look I can't quite make out. "You model too, don't you?"

"Yes, but I'm not doing as many shows anymore. I want to focus on running my club."

"Fair enough." A successful, sexy, rich woman would intimidate most men. Not me—I think running a business just makes her more appealing. It's a nice change to hang out with a woman who's driven and motivated to do something with her life. I want to know everything about her and what makes her tick.

"What do you do?" she asks.

I point to the patch on my vest. "Vice president of the best motorcycle club in the US."

She smiles. "I know that, but what else do you do as a job?"

My shoulders tense. Her father, Garrett, and brother Alec know we grow, distribute, and sell large amounts of pot and aren't licensed. Hell, they said we could. Nothing goes on in the town without her father's say-so, but I don't know how much she knows, so I decide to talk about the charity.

"We help with Zara's charity, at the women and children's safe house."

Her face lights up. "It's unbelievable. Zara has done such a good job. After everything she's been through, she's turned a devastating outcome into something positive. So… what's your role in it?"

"We renovated the property and building where the charity houses the women and children. We help the victims, like picking them up and taking them away from dangerous situations they're in and bringing them to the charity." I think back to the frightened woman and children we picked up last week. "It's really brought the club together, everyone working together to help others. We're honored to assist, and the town's response to us has been positive." People now smile and praise us for helping rather than fearing us.

She steps closer to me and searches my eyes. "You're doing such a great job. I'm proud of you and everyone who's helped Zara."

She's proud of me? I don't think anyone has said that to me before. I give her one of my panty-dropping smiles.

She lifts her hands and grabs each side of my leather cut. "You look sexy in leather."

I'm the one who's supposed to be dishing out compliments. Maybe… just maybe… I'm in over my head with her.

I slip my arms out of my cut and hold it out for her, and without hesitation, she slides the leather vest on over her red dress. My mouth goes dry. Fuck meeeeeee! "Hmm… Temptress, you look better." My voice is husky, and my hard-on is achingly uncomfortable against my jeans. An ol' lady property patch with my name on it would be even better.

I glance at the men to see if anyone noticed. Bomber's shaking his head at me, and Axle's jaw is gaping. We don't let just anyone wear our club colors. No man outside the MC is allowed to wear our patch, and only the women we're serious about—our ol' ladies—get to wear a property patch with their man's name on it. By letting Sophie wear my cut, I know Axle is going to give me shit later for it.

I lean toward Sophie, pulling her blond wavy hair from under my cut and allowing it to fall down her back, while she gives me a slow once-over.

Harrison appears next to us and hands me my beer. "Thanks," I say, wishing I hadn't asked for it now.

"Where's my drink?" Sophie asks Harrison.

"Sorry, sis, you should have told me beforehand."

"Well… I might go over and order a cocktail. I'll be back soon," she says as she makes her way over to the bar, swaying those sexy hips. I stare at her, captivated.

Harrison's laugh brings my eyes back to him. "I almost feel bad for you."

I frown. "What do you mean?"

"It looks like Sophie's got her eye on you."

I chuckle. "I'm stoked with that." I peek at her again. She's at the bar and is flanked by a man on either side, undoubtedly trying to buy her a drink. Annoyance flares up inside of me. She's *mine* for tonight.

"I thought you were a one-night-stand type of guy."

I am, apart from Candy. "Why do you say that?" I ask.

"Well… you're looking at my sister like you want to be her knight in shining armor. Sophie can more than handle herself with men, but proceed with caution. Every man has wanted to bang her, and after one night, every one of them has wanted more from her. But she doesn't have any more to give, and if she sees you getting jealous or needy"—he looks at her, then at me, and I assume he means the way I'm acting now—"she will run. She's a player."

"What makes you think I want anything other than sex?"

He mocks me with his laughter.

"What?" I ask him.

"She's wearing your cut. She's already got you by the balls."

I chuckle but don't reply because Sophie comes over to us.

She tugs at my arm. "Come have a shot with me."

I smile back at her. "Sure, darlin'."

Harrison gives me an I-told-you-so grin.

I follow Sophie to the bar, where the barman ignores all the other patrons, only talking to Sophie. "Your cocktail is being made now." He tilts his head to the lady mixing a blue drink in a fancy glass beside him. "Do you want anything else?" he asks, then licks his lips, his eyes flicking to her breasts, then back to her face.

I itch to say something, but I want Sophie in my bed badly, so I don't want to screw it up.

She gives him a naughty smile. "Two tequila shots, please." The man pulls out the shot glasses, pours the clear liquid into them, and puts the glasses in front of us. "Can we have lime and salt?" she asks. The barman obliges.

"Give me your hand," my little temptress demands. I follow her command. She dips her fingers into a drink and dabs tequila on the part of my hand between my thumb and index finger.

I watch as she shakes salt onto my wet skin. *She's not, is she…* Sophie bends down and runs her soft tongue along the edge of my hand, taking the salt with her, then she tosses her drink back. The movement is erotic.

Sophie places the lime between my lips, making my heart pound. She leans toward me, and her mouth presses against mine as she sucks the lime. My mouth waters—it's intoxicating. She seductively licks her lips. I swiftly down my shot, feeling the warmth of the alcohol, but my attention stays fixed on Sophie.

The barwoman places the cocktail in front of her. "Can I have two more tequila shots?" I ask. She gives me the once-over and then a flirty smile, so I smile back. As soon as the barwoman pours one shot, I take Sophie's hand in mine, dab my fingers into the liquid and dampen her hand, then shake the salt. My body hums in anticipation.

I bring her hand to my lip, and sensually lick the salt while maintaining eye contact. I delight in watching her eyes heat and those luscious lips part. I bring the glass to my lips and finish the shot, but instead of the lime, my hand goes to Sophie's chin. I lean down, sealing my mouth over hers. Sophie's lips are soft. I apply a gentle pressure to begin with, and she kisses me back. As my tongue dips inside, I taste her with long, leisurely licks.

Her hands rise, looping over my shoulders until she's running her fingers through my hair. My heartbeat is surging as the kiss deepens. I press my lips against hers harder but try to rein in my wild passion. My hands slip to her hips, then the curve of her ass. The club evaporates, and all that's left is us. I break the kiss, then yank her hips toward mine. I slowly grind my pelvis against hers so that she can feel my hard-on.

Hunger burns in her eyes, proof that I'm not the only one who's turned on. I lean over and run my nose up her throat to her ear, noticing her breathing quicken. I place two kisses on her neck. "I can't wait to fuck you," I tell her, my voice rough.

She squirms. Goosebumps travel along her arms. *She likes the dirty talk.* My fingers dig into her sides. I want her now… to explore every inch of her. She slips her hand between us and grabs my dick through my jeans. I jerk and a hiss escapes me. She slowly rubs up and down, making my eyes roll back.

She bites down on her plump red bottom lip. "I'm ready for round one now," she purrs, and I let out a drawn-out groan. No shyness… just a woman who knows what she wants. I want to brand my name on her pretty little flesh and keep her all for myself.

"Four more shots of tequila," I say to the bartender. I'm already having fun with her. I don't want this night to end. With the two of us drunk together, the night is going to be wild.

I can't believe a man hasn't put a ring on her finger yet. She's the ultimate catch. I wonder what it would take for her to stay at the clubhouse with me and get to know me. Hell, if given the chance, I could show her I'm a decent guy and maybe, just maybe, I'd be worthy.

THREE
MY NAME IS SOPHIE YOUNG NOW

Sophie

A familiar phone is ringing. My hands scour the bed searching for it, but instead I touch a warm body and hear a deep moan. *Oh shit!* My eyes fly open and I sit up, but everything aches. My mouth is dry and tastes like crap. I look around and see my dress, which has been thrown haphazardly on the floor, along with his jeans and shirt.

My phone is lighting up on the floor. I lean down to pick it up, to see a gold ring on my wedding finger. My hand whips to my mouth and I gag. What the hell happened last night?

I stare down at my phone to see Alec's name. "Hello," I answer in a hoarse voice.

"We're not waiting all day for you. I'll give you one hour, or you can catch a lift home with the biker you married."

My world spins… *biker*… I cringe… *married*… My eyes bulge out of my head. "Are you serious?" I ask as vomit creeps up my throat again. "I think I'm going to be sick."

Someone is laughing in the background of the call. "Give me the phone." It's Harrison.

"Hey, sis. How's the head?"

"Am I really married?" I ask, praying for a different answer.

"Didn't you notice the ring on your finger?"

"I did. Is it a fake?" *Wishful thinking.*

"Oh, no… it's legit. Viper made sure it was."

Pausing, I remember flirting with him, being attracted to his charming personality, and wearing his vest. I remember the shots and the thrill of being with a bad-boy biker who oozed sexual energy. I knew I wanted to screw him, but after the shots and the flirting, everything else is a blank.

"I never black out; I must have been drunk." Irritation flares. "Why didn't you stop me from getting married if you knew I was drunk?"

He laughs. "Sophie, no one can stop you when you have your mind set on something, and I knew you could get a divorce, so who cares? It was a bit of fun."

"Fun!" The word tastes like poison on my tongue. "Where was Alec?" I didn't think he would let me go through with it.

"He left hours before your very touching ceremony."

As I peek at Viper, I say, "God! I married the guy and I don't even know his real first name. What's the marriage certificate say? Sophie Crown and Viper?" My stomach rolls again. I've worked so hard to get where I am today. My reputation is important to me, and now everyone will find out I married a biker in Vegas. I curse myself.

Harrison laughs. "It's Brayden Young, and *you* are Sophie Young now."

I slap a hand over my face and inhale deeply through my nose. This is my worst nightmare. Viper… or rather Brayden… *whatever his name is…* is facing away from me. But from the muscles in his back and the way his bicep is bulging as it covers his face, I can't deny his yumminess. My eyes focus on the way the sheet half-covers his perfect, round ass. I almost want to wake him up to give myself something to remember him by, but I shake my head. I need to get my shit together.

"Well, I'd better go and organize a lift, then message the lawyer on my way." I hang up on my annoying brother, who's laughing again.

Marriage. I want to curl up into a ball and die. I carefully slide over and off the bed.

My eyes scan the room for my thong, but it's nowhere to be seen. I tiptoe over to my dress, aware of the throb of last night between my legs. I lift the dress up and over my head, pulling it down to where it fits.

I peer around to see my bag by the table near the front door. I glance back at him one last time. Well… I clearly had a blast. I desperately wish I could at least recall the night, but then I recoil. *Nope, probably better that I don't.*

When I walk over to the door, I grasp my bag, sling it over my shoulder, gently open the door, and walk outside before quietly closing the door behind me. Light floods the corridor. I dash past, hoping no one I know will see my walk of shame.

After I get out of the elevator, I pull out my phone and call the private limousine company we hired. "It's Sophie Crown. Can you come and pick me up? I'm at, uh…" I peer around at the establishment until I reach reception and read the wording. "I'm at Caesar's Palace."

"I'll be there in ten minutes," the man replies.

"Thank you." The ten minutes couldn't come soon enough.

As my hand falls to my side, I catch a glimpse of something on my wrist, so I lift my arm closer to my eyes to inspect it. "Oh… fuck off…" I say aloud. A woman glares at me as she walks past. The words "Partner in Crime" are tattooed across my wrist. I attempt to rub at it, but it's tender and there's smeared ink around it. I'd bet Viper has a similar tattoo on him. I've never wanted a tattoo. What the hell happened last night?

I bow my head, worried that the bikers or their women will see me. I spot a lounge chair, so I hurry over and take a seat. My stomach rolls, and I hang my head, placing my hand over half of my face to hide. I go to my messages and search for Piper's name, and when it comes up, I dial her.

"Hello," she answers.

"I'm coming back home to New York."

"What happened?"

My mouth opens to speak, but I don't think I can even say the words. "I screwed up… big time!"

I have never packed my bags as hastily as I did when I got back to the resort. On the flight back to New York, I have vivid flashbacks of that night, of his lips ravishing my body and the overwhelming ecstasy that engulfed me. Once I arrive home, the driver carries my suitcase up the elevator and to my apartment. I swipe my key, and the front door unlocks.

"Where would you like the suitcase, ma'am?"

"Inside my bedroom."

I head to the coffee machine. I set down a cup and press the button. My body desperately needs caffeine.

"Hello," Piper says behind me. I turn to her.

My best friend is stunning. Long, straight brown hair, brown eyes, and olive skin. Naturally beautiful. She should model with me but prefers to work an office job as an executive assistant to a CEO. As she walks to the fridge, she asks, "Do you need any milk while I'm here?"

"No, thank you. It's an espresso for me this morning."

She takes out the milk, ready for the mocha she has every morning.

When my cup has been filled, I breathe in the heavenly scent, then bring the cup to my lips and take a sip of the hot, bitter drink.

Piper's eyes go to my hand, then bulge. "I can't believe you got married."

I let out a long groan. "Me too."

Her lips press into a thin line. "It's so unlike you. You must have been really drunk. I'm a little disappointed I missed out."

"You didn't miss anything, and anyway, I'm already organizing the divorce papers."

"He must be hot."

I take another sip, then grin over the edge of my cup. "He's gorgeous. Like the full bad-boy swagger, but his swoon-worthy smile had my panties wet."

Her head falls back as she laughs. "Have you got a photo? I need to see this fine specimen before you divorce him."

"I haven't even looked." I walk over and place my coffee on the table before I go to my room to find my phone in my bag. I go through my photos as I make my way back to Piper.

I come across a photo of me and Viper smiling. He has his arm around me, and our hands are up showing our wedding rings. I'm slightly taken aback by the happiness shining from me in this picture, even though my eyes appear glazed. I turn my phone around and show it to Piper, who takes it from me to get a better look.

"He's handsome. His beard is perfectly manicured and his hair is neat, except for the unruly piece that falls near his eyes, which is very sexy, may I add. It's such a turn-on when a man takes proper care of himself," I say.

"What's his body like?" she asks.

I try to think back. "His body was hard, and he had a six-pack."

"At least you didn't marry a slob with a beer belly. He looks after himself, so you two have that in common," she says as she passes me my phone. I place it on the freestanding charger by the wall on the counter.

"True…" I answer while remembering him undressing me with his eyes. "Oh, Piper, he's something else." I do a chef's kiss. "From his sexy deep voice to his hard body." I sigh. "We couldn't keep our hands off each other. It was a good night… well, from what I can remember."

I take a seat and bring my cup to my mouth again.

"Are you still going to the gym today?" Piper asks.

"Considering all the calories I had, I have to."

"I might join you. How was the get-together, anyway? Did you see Zara and Knox? How's Zara doing?"

"Knox's nickname is Bomber. It took me a while to get my head around it, but Knox and Zara were good. Knox was glued to her all night. Even when us women were dancing, he wasn't too far away. It's sweet that they got back together. Zara's been through hell. She's so strong."

Piper takes her coffee, walks over, and sits next to me. She cringes and then asks, "How were the other women?"

I don't have many female friends—it's just me and Piper in New York.

"They were quiet… I thought they were going to be loud, bitchy women. They were far from it. Ava, the one with the War Brothers MC president, apologized to people when she accidentally bumped into them while dancing." I laugh, thinking back to that. "Elena was nice too. That's Ava's sister; she's with another MC member, Axle. The banter between those two was hilarious."

Piper's eyes are wide as she stirs her coffee. "Next time

you'll have to invite me. What did you say to your sexy husband before you left?"

I flinch. "I didn't say anything."

She laughs. "What do you mean you didn't say anything? You just left your husband in bed and did a runner?"

"Pretty much. It's not like normal, where a guy slept over and I kicked him out the next morning. Viper knew who I was and what I did because it was a family event. I was in uncharted waters, with a ring on my finger."

"How was the sex?" Piper asks.

"I woke up sore, and my vajayjay was tender. The flash-backs I've been getting…" I fan my face. "So hot!"

Her grin stretches wide. "That's another positive… What did your brothers say about getting married?" she asks.

"Harrison and Lawson were amused."

She quirks a brow. "And Alec?"

I roll my eyes. "He told me how irresponsible I was. He didn't need to rub it in." I frown. "I've tried so hard over the years to prove to my family I'm more than just a model."

Her face falls. She puts a hand on my leg. "You're so much more than just a model. You don't have to prove your worth to anyone."

FOUR
BLACKMAIL NEVER TASTED SO GOOD

Viper

I SWIPE MY HAND OVER MY SWEATY FOREHEAD. I'M PANTING AS I step back into the house with Rage after our morning run. When my phone beeps, Sophie's name is on the screen. This must be message number two hundred thirty-one, and I already know what it's going to say before I open it. *Sign the divorce papers blah blah blah.* Rage walks over to the fridge and passes me a bottle of cold water. I twist the cap off and gulp down the cool fluid.

I let out a sigh. "I needed that."

Candy dashes over to me and rubs a hand down my chest and my abs. As horny as I am, I take a step back, pulling my shirt out of the hem of my shorts and slipping it back on. Candy looks away, then steps over to me and stands on her toes to whisper in my ear. "You must be horny; we haven't had sex since you left for Vegas."

I chuckle. "I am, but…" I lift my hand up, showing my wedding ring.

Candy stiffens. "It means nothing, though. Doesn't she want you to sign the divorce papers?"

I don't know how my marriage is the topic of conversation around here. I shrug indifferently. Wifey can email, call, message threatening me as much as she wants with divorce papers, but I ain't signing shit till she gets her sweet ass back to Crown Village so that I can talk to her face to face. "I'm still married, and until I get a divorce, I'm not cheating." Who knew… me married, ha! She was the woman everyone wanted. I was the lucky son of a bitch who conned her into being my wife.

Candy sighs. "But you're not really in a relationship, so how is it cheating?"

Technically, she's probably right, but on the slight chance I have a shot with Sophie, I'm not doing anything that might screw that up. "I like Sophie, so I'm not risking it." I'm honest with Candy, but it's like my words never penetrate.

"Oh…" Her mouth curves down and her body droops.

I cup her chin and lift her face so that her eyes meet mine. She's a lovely gal… she's just not for me. "Don't frown, pretty girl. There are other single guys here."

Candy takes a step away from me and fakes a smile before walking off. I can't help but feel bad for her, even though I told her we weren't serious. Maybe I shouldn't have slept with her for so long. I guess the change from the person I was before Vegas to who I am now, suddenly married and loyal to my wife who I spent one night with, has been drastic.

"Don't feel guilty," Rage says.

I run a hand through my hair. "I told Candy it was casual. Heck, I've slept with other people, and she never said anything."

"Maybe she thought she was going to be *the one*."

I shake my head. "She never listens to me. There are other

guys here. Why don't you spend some time with her? You're single."

He takes a step back, lifting his hands in protest. "No... I don't want the drama."

"You haven't liked anyone since Ashton's girlfriend Mia." Rage got into a fight with Ashton over a chick. Ashton used to fight in our illegal fighting ring but quit because he fell in love.

Rage's eyes narrow slightly. "I didn't know they were together when I liked Mia and, again... I don't want drama. I'm happy fighting in the ring and doing what I have to for the club. What are you going to do about your wife?"

That puts a grin back on my face. "I'm waiting for Sophie to come back to see me in person. Judging from the daily messages and phone calls, I sense it will happen soon."

"You scored with her. She's a ten."

She's way too good for me. "I know I did." I'm proud to call her my wife.

"How'd you get her to marry you?"

"It was a wild night. Plenty of drinking, flirting, and dancing. The sex and everything else was..." I let out a low whistle, thinking back to that night. "Sweetest pussy I've ever tasted."

"How did being with her one night make you change?"

I drift off, thinking. "I've never craved to get to know a woman like I have with her. I guess drunk me figured getting hitched was my best chance at hanging on to her." The thought makes me swallow hard. I could be setting myself up for failure, but I think she's worth the risk.

I walk outside to see Zara and Bomber at the table with Reaper, Elena, and Axle. As I get closer, Axle turns to me, and his eyes light up. I can already tell he's going to be a smartass.

"You signed those divorce papers yet?" Axle asks.

My lips curve up into a wide smile. "No..."

Bomber shakes his head at me. "I thought Alec would be on your case about divorcing, but he told me Sophie dug her grave—she can get herself out of it. Their father, Garrett, is a different matter. No one has told him yet, so I'd just sign them and get it over with. He's a prick and can cause problems..." Bomber looks at Reaper. "Problems for everyone."

"You know how persuasive I am, and I'm sure her father will want her to stay in Crown Village with him."

"Yours is going down as the shortest marriage in the MC's history."

"We'll see," I snap back confidently at Axle.

He chuckles, and when I stand next to him, he whacks my back. "What are you going to do?"

"As I said to Rage inside, Sophie has to come back here so that I can talk to her face to face."

He searches my eyes. "What exactly are you planning to do? Hold her hostage?"

Just the thought of her being back makes my heart pump faster, sending a thrill through my body. "Bondage isn't my thing... that's Cash's. I'm going to make Sophie an offer she can't refuse."

My phone rings in my back pocket. I pull it out to see Sophie calling.

"Hello, wifey," I tease. There are chuckles around the table.

Sophie growls. "I'm not your wife!"

"The marriage certificate says otherwise," I say through a smile, thoroughly enjoying this back and forth between us. I'm stubborn, and I won't budge.

"Because you won't sign the divorce papers." Her voice gets higher toward the end.

"Oh, well... I told you my conditions."

"Oh... I know. Luckily, I'm on my way to Crown Village.

I'll be at the clubhouse tonight with the divorce papers, so you had better keep your word and sign it."

My smile grows… *I don't think so…*

There's a War Brothers MC party on. The music is pumping, and we're sitting around the fire, enjoying the warmth, drinking, with the flames high in the air. Elena and Axle, Reaper and Ava, and Zara and Bomber are all out together as couples, so it's just us single boys and the sweet butts hanging out.

"Viper," Twitch calls out.

"Yeah," I reply.

He looks down at his phone, then back at me. "There's a limousine out front. I assume it's your wife." Twitch has the security system linked up to his phone.

A shiver makes its way down my back. I've never experienced this level of anxiety around a woman before. I put down my beer. *It's showtime!*

I go in the back door and stride through the house. I'm in time to see her walk through the front door. She has dark blue jeans on that fit her like a glove and a tightly fitted shirt that's short enough to see an inch of that perfect skin between her shirt and jeans. She has a manilla folder in her hand.

When her eyes land on me, they sharpen like a blade.

I give her my best panty-dropping smile. "Hey, wifey, it's good to see you." Because holy hell, it is.

The ice in her veins melts just a little and her body loses some of its stiffness. She gives me the once-over, and I don't miss the heat in her eyes. This may be easier than I thought.

She holds up the folder in one hand and a pen in the other. "Is there a table where you can sign this?"

The fact she even brought the pen with her is amusing.

I gesture toward the interior of the house. "This way," I say as I allow her to go first. Her shoulders are back and her head held high—her confidence and the way she holds herself is another sexy thing about her. I have to adjust myself as I walk behind her.

She slowly walks through as if examining the clubhouse, then makes her way over to our large wooden dining table. Her fingers caress the wood before she puts the folder down. "This table is exquisite," she points out. I know what is exquisite, and it isn't the table.

Sophie opens the folder, pulls out the stapled papers, and places them in front of me. "Where the green tab is poking out is where you sign, and here's your ring back," she says, placing the ring on top of the papers.

I ignore her and step toward her. I lean in while inhaling deeply through my nose. Her hair smells fruity. She doesn't move away from me. She holds her ground, those big blue eyes glancing up at me quizzically.

"I love the smell of your hair."

She cocks her head. "It's my hair treatment… the scent is apple."

"Whatever it is, I want to bottle it up."

She playfully whacks my chest, and I take a step back, chuckling. "Stop flirting with me. Sign the papers," she demands. I love the feistiness in her, but her tone doesn't sound convincing.

My eyes seductively roam her body. "I'm allowed to flirt with *my* wife."

She picks up the papers from the table and shoves them into my chest, and I watch as the ring tumbles to the ground. I raise my arms, refusing to touch the papers.

"Brayden, you said you would. Now keep your word!"

No one uses my real name, though I like her saying it. "No can do, wifey."

The hand holding the papers falls, and she glares daggers. "You made me travel back to Crown Village so that you could say no to signing the papers?"

The thrill of seeing her so revved up makes my pulse quicken. I lean in close to her again, my mouth brushing her ear. "You're sexy when you're mad."

Her breath hitches, and I'm having way too much fun with this. "I'll sign the papers if you stay with me in the clubhouse for a month." I wish I could ask for longer, but I thought one month would be pushing it.

Her eyes widen, and those plump lips gape open. "A month?"

I give her a sharp nod. There's this small part of me that knows this arrangement has the potential to cause problems, but the large part, my dick included, says fuck it. That's a future me problem. "That's my condition. One entire month with me, in my bed, at the clubhouse. If you still don't want to remain married after that, I'll sign the papers." One month to seal the deal. I'm persuasive. I think I've got this.

She looks away, as if considering my offer. "I own a business in New York. I can't just stay with you because you want to play games." Her mouth says no, but her eyes sparkle.

"Oh, come on, temptress. You're already here in Crown Village. I'm sure you can work from your laptop or phone or whatever you used last time you were here."

She shakes her head. "No… it's not happening."

"It's not like you have many other options. Your family lives here, so it can't be that bad, right?"

She pauses. *Yes!* I keep my face passive, but inside I'm cheering.

"One month is a long time. You seem confident I'll stay married to you, or do you just want to sleep with me again?"

"Both," I reply with no hesitation. "But while you're here, you're not allowed to sleep with or kiss or be involved with any other man. I want to be greedy and selfish with you." I needed to make that clear because she's mine for a whole month. *Mine, mine, mine, mine, mine.*

A naughty smile curves on her lips. "What makes you think you can handle me for a month?"

The thrill of having her in my bed shoots straight to my dick. "Aww, wifey…" I say huskily, "I'm game if you are."

She bites her lip and her eyes dart away.

"At least have a drink with me. You've come all this way. What's the rush?"

Her face is blank, and it makes me think she's going to turn me down, but then she glares at me. "One drink," she warns.

Sophie

I curse myself as I walk through the house. I'm not sure what it is about Viper that makes me say yes. His arrogant and cocky smile? His relentlessness to have me? It isn't cringeworthy like the men back in New York; instead, it has awakened a part of me that lights up every time I talk to him. I find myself stupidly smiling, so I shake my head to try to rid myself of those thoughts, but instead my eyes go to Viper's ass. Those jeans hug him so incredibly well.

I refuse to be the woman who pines for a man, but goddamn, I'm so attracted to him. From the confident, sexy swagger in his walk to the way his shirt fits snugly over his broad shoulders to that War Brothers MC vest, I like it all. I should run far, far away from him, but it seems I have no self-restraint. I blame the jeans.

He grabs a small bottle from the fridge and hands it to me. "Is this vodka drink okay, or do you want something else?"

I peer down at the bottle with the brightly colored label. "It's fine," I reply as I take it from him.

Viper's lips tip into a charming smile. He opens the back door and steps outside but keeps the door open for me to pass through. I raise a brow suspiciously at his gentleman act. The music is loud, with a heavy-metal beat. The night is dark apart from the fire people are sitting around.

Viper grabs my hand in his, links our fingers together, and pulls me toward everyone. I startle at first but follow his lead. My heart beats faster at the affectionate gesture.

When we reach the men and women, conversations pause and heads turn to us. Everyone is scattered around the fire, and with that and the dark sky, it's difficult to make out each person's face.

The closest men to us have women on their laps. A young man is seated to the right with a woman with pigtails. They keep staring at me with wide eyes.

The man to my left has a friendly smile on his face. He tips his beer up to me in greeting. He has on a black bracelet and rings on his fingers. I lift my bottle back, then they return to their discussions. I glance around again to find someone I know.

"Zara and Bomber aren't here. They most likely won't be back till late."

My shoulders fall. I wanted to see them again. I've missed them… well, I've missed all my family. Being back in Crown Village has brought me and my brothers closer again. Every time I return to New York from Crown Village, I'm on a downer for days.

I bring the bottle to my lips again and take a longer drink. "Are you okay?"

I subtly shake my head to get out of my daydream, then I

study him. He has curved brows. My cheeks heat at being overly emotional. "So, this is what a famous War Brothers MC clubhouse party looks like," I say sarcastically. I glance around and shake my head. "It's very tame. I'm disappointed."

Viper laughs. "The strippers come out later, but feel free to get the party started," he says and then adds a cheeky wink.

I giggle. *Smooth… real smooth.* It's never a dull moment when he's around. I sense Viper's eyes on me as I bring the bottle to my lips. After taking a drink, I tease my tongue out, letting it glide across my bottom lip, savoring the last remaining drops of the sugary drink.

Suddenly, I'm being lifted, which makes me squeal. Then he brings me onto his lap. His arms encircle me, holding me tightly. I'm filled with warmth. I breathe in deep and smell his cologne. It's a tropical scent of coconut and lime, and it reminds me of the beach.

"Have you missed me, wifey?"

I chuckle and shift so that I can see him. "No, I haven't."

"I think you have."

Even though the alcohol tainted my choices, from what I remember, Zara and Knox's bachelorette and bachelor party was a fun night. It was good to let my hair down with my brothers, Zara, Knox, and the MC.

"Do you want me to help you pack your bags tomorrow?"

I raise a brow at him and purse my lips.

"I know you want to," he purrs.

"Oh really?" I ask sarcastically. "What makes you think that?"

"You. Are. Bored."

I huff. "I'm actually very busy." I don't have much time to myself.

"You're bored with your routine and your perfect life."

A tinge of annoyance strikes me, even though there may

be some truth to it. "You don't know me!"

His expression darkens. His fingertips graze my arm, feather-like, from my shoulder slowly down to my wrist, making my body shudder from only his touch. He smirks devilishly, savoring the reaction he's extracting from me.

He lowers his head so that our faces are only inches apart. His eyes burn into mine. "I'd like to get to know you," he says in a tone that's both seductive and a breathy plea.

I briefly think I should pull away, but the other ninety-nine percent of me is screaming not to. I focus on his full lips, and my self-control disappears. I lean in, close my eyes, and bring my lips to his. He kisses back hard. As our mouths move in sync, his tongue seeks entry. I don't deny him. I meet his tongue, melting into him.

My arms slither over his shoulders and to the back of his neck as our tongues whirl feverishly together. He groans, and it vibrates right through me. The ache between my legs comes hard and fast. He takes from my mouth, greedily… possessively. My body overheats as the passion increases in intensity.

He pulls me closer to him, our tongues dueling fiercely, taking what we want. My heart thumps as he devours me, but then he retreats and I'm left breathless and yearning for more. He tugs my arms from his shoulders, then takes my left hand in his while his other hand goes to his pocket. He pulls out my wedding ring and slides it back onto my ring finger.

"Stay with me for one month. You never know—you might enjoy yourself."

I know I will. One month with a sexy biker and extra time with my family… It's not a terrible idea. My resolve vanishes and my body buzzes as I half laugh at being reckless… again! "Okay," I answer him. "I'll stay."

Viper's lips curve up into a wicked grin as his eyes dance with victory.

FIVE

LET'S PLAY A GAME

Sophie

"Yes, I know I'm an idiot."

Lawson chuckles. "Why does Viper get under your skin? Any other man you'd be telling to go F himself, so why is he different?"

It's morning, and I chuck the third shot of whiskey down my throat and slam the glass on the table. I feel like an alcoholic, but desperate times call for desperate measures. "First, I never married any other guy, so there was no obligation to stick around."

His eyes narrow. "Don't bullshit. Our lawyer would find a way to get you out of the marriage without his signature."

I flinch. I've come to talk to Lawson because he's smart and levelheaded. Lawson is right. I break eye contact and shrug lazily. "I don't know… maybe it will be fun." I haven't experienced a rush of excitement in a long time.

"How are you going to go living out in the wilderness?"

I shiver. "What do you mean, the wilderness?" The clubhouse seemed out of the way, but I guess I wasn't too interested in the surroundings when I first went there. All I wanted was for Viper to sign the divorce papers.

"The MC is on the edge of the national park. You have to take a gravel road to even get out there. Going from the city to the wilderness is going to be a dramatic change, don't you think?"

I gulp heavily. "Nothing I can't handle," I say with confidence, even though I certainly don't feel it.

He chuckles louder this time. "I give you a week… Think bears, raccoons, coyotes, mountain lions… should I go on?"

I shake my head. "You've made your point. The men in the MC are tough… they'll protect me." *Well… they'd better.*

"Have you told Dad yet?"

Just the thought of him knowing has me filling up another shot. "No."

"If he doesn't know already, he will find out."

I toss the drink back; the burn lessens with every shot. "I don't need the lecture… yes, I screwed up. I know it."

"When's the one month start?"

"I'm going there today. Oh… that reminds me." I grab my phone from the kitchen counter and search the internet for a local retail store. I call the store, and when an employee answers, I say, "I want the best bed you have available. Price isn't an issue, but I need it delivered today." I give my card information to pay for it.

Lawson has a big smile on his face. "What?" I ask him.

"You're really doing this, aren't you?"

I sharply bob my head. "I'd better call the family limousine to take me shopping. I'll have to buy more clothes."

As I'm leaving, Lawson calls out, "Sophie!"

I glance behind me.

"Nice tattoo."

I bring my wrist up to my face and glare at it. Lawson laughs as I storm out.

After shopping and filling the limousine's trunk with bags of clothes, I decide to take some time out and relax by the beach, under a palm tree. I watch as the water drifts back and forth across the sand.

Being in Crown Village is going to be a breeze. All I have to do is stay at the MC for one month. I seem to get along with the women. The beaches are beautiful here, and I'm enjoying spending time with my brothers. I miss Lawson's advice and our chats, and I miss Harrison's personality, which always puts a smile on my face. And Alec... I chuckle. No... I haven't missed him. I love him—he's my brother. But he's too uptight. I've always been closer to Lawson and Harrison than him.

As the limousine crawls along the gravel road, toward the clubhouse, flutters fill my stomach and gradually get worse. In the meantime, I call Maddy, the manager of my club, and tell her I'll be working remotely from Crown Village.

The road is lined with trees and lush plants. It's a nice change compared to the busy, hectic life in New York. When we reach the driveway, we stop outside a large gate, which effortlessly opens for us. We glide through.

The clubhouse looks like a large two-level country-style home. The chauffeur opens the back door for me, and as I step out, Viper walks out with a cocky grin and that sexy swagger. I'm not sure whether I want to kiss him or throttle him for putting me in this position.

"Hey, wifey, do you need help with your bags?"

I roll my eyes at him. "Yes, they're in the back."

He wanders over to the open trunk and laughs, so I walk over to see what's so funny.

"How many clothes do you own?"

I frown. "What… it's not that much. I purchased most of them today."

He points to my pillows. "I own pillows, you know."

I cringe, imagining how old and gross they would be. "I like heaps of pillows on my bed. You wanted me here, so you can't whine now, and anyway, I doubt your pillowcases have a high thread count like these do."

He gives me an odd look, and I realize he has no clue what I'm talking about.

"I like plenty of pillows and luxury pillowcases and bedsheets."

He nods slowly, dragging out the motion, though he's smothering a laugh. With his hands full of my bags, he leads the way through the front door and the hallway to an open-plan living space where there's a large dining room, and further along is a pool table. To the back right, I can see couches and a large flat-screen. As I walk along, I see closed doors to the left. I keep going until there's a set of stairs that lead to the next level.

"Where is everyone?" It seems too quiet.

"Outside having lunch."

I follow him up the stairs to a long hallway with a mix of closed and open doors, which I assume are bedrooms. "In here," he says as he opens a door. When I walk in, I'm hit with the heady smell of his cologne. His room is basic, with white walls and what seems to be a king-size bed with a black leather frame, flanked by gloss-black bedside tables.

I can do this. It could be much worse.

Viper places my bags beside the bed and observes me. "Does it meet your standards?"

The side of my lips curve up. "I guess so," I joke and point to the bed. "I ordered a king-size bed. It should arrive today."

"You ordered a bed?" he repeats as if surprised.

I give him a sassy grin. "I don't want to catch an STD or something."

His head falls back as he laughs. "You're really something, aren't you?"

"I've been warned about your womanizing ways," I say, amused.

"And they warned me about your… ways."

I shrug. "I'm busy and I like sex."

He nods. "Me too!"

I study him. God, he's handsome. Strong, square jaw, and I do love a good beard. The confidence and sexual energy that radiate from him also add to his appeal. I'm usually a great judge of character. How did I not see the devil in disguise?

The chauffeur walks in with my suitcase. "I'll go back down and help him get the rest of your bags," Viper says, and they leave together, leaving me alone in the room.

At least his bed is made, and as I make my way to his wardrobe and slide the door open, I see he has hung up all his clothes fairly neatly. Well… thank the Lord, he's clean. There's no sign of dirty clothes lying around, and it smells heavenly… so far, so good. My heart is still beating fast as I wonder what is waiting for me around every corner.

Viper walks in with his hands full and places the bags beside the others. He's not breathing heavily or even breaking a sweat, unlike the chauffeur.

"Ma'am, do you need anything else?"

"No, thank you." I give him a small smile before he leaves.

Viper peers down, and when I follow his gaze, he's staring at my wedding ring. "Yes, I'm still wearing it." He needs to think I'm giving this so-called marriage a chance so at the end, he will sign those papers.

"Good! You can't half-ass this. I want you to give us a shot… you never know, you could grow to love me." His voice carries both flirtation and a touch of hopefulness. I *almost* feel guilty knowing that I'll be out of here as soon as the four weeks are up.

"And what's this, hmmm?" I ask, raising my hand and turning it, showing him my wrist. Oh, the smugness in his eyes makes me want to slap that look right off his face. He turns his wrist over and I see the same "Partner in Crime" tattoo.

"We got tattoos… we got married… is there anything else I should know about?" Sarcasm laces my tone.

"I've got some photos of us if you want to see?"

My head inches back. "No." I don't need to see any more evidence of that night, and now I have to organize laser tattoo removal.

I break eye contact and gaze around the room. "Where's the bathroom?"

His eyes go to the doorway. "Down the hallway and to the left."

My stomach sinks. "You don't have your own bathroom?" I don't think I've ever had to share a bathroom before.

He must see the disturbed look on my face. "Don't stress. The women clean them every couple of days." My eyes bulge. *Cleaning…* I hope he isn't expecting me to clean toilets and bathrooms. It provides a small bit of relief that they're clean, but I'm still not happy with the arrangement.

"Are you hungry?" he asks.

I nod. I guess I could eat. He tilts his head toward the door with the sexy half-grin that always seems to be etched on his face. "Come outside for lunch and see everyone."

"Sure… you go down. I need to make a phone call."

He tilts his chin up at me, and once he's gone, I pull my phone out and dial Piper.

"Hey," she answers in an upbeat voice. "How did the divorce go?"

I cringe. "Well… I'm staying here in Crown Village at the clubhouse for a month."

"What?" she squeaks. "How did he convince you to do that?"

I exhale heavily through my mouth. "Viper's blackmailing me. If I stay with him at the clubhouse for a month and I still don't want to be with him, then he'll sign the papers."

"I'm just shocked…" She pauses. "And worried… with him you're reckless. But I guess you could just be really into him."

She's not the only one who's shocked. I'm surprised at my own actions. I smile at the thought of him. "He's gorgeous, and I'm loving the bad-boy biker vibes. I thought I'd walk into a dirty old clubhouse, but it's like a large two-story country house. The clubhouse is tidy, from what I've seen so far." There's a moment of silence. "Piper?"

"I'm here. A month is a long time… I'm going to miss you."

"I'm going to miss you too. Can you do me a favor? I'll send you a message with the clubhouse address, but can you courier out my laptop and charger? I thought I was only going to be here for a day or so. That's no longer the case."

"I can do that."

"Thank you. I'd better go. Viper wants me to meet everyone again. This should be interesting…"

She laughs. "Have fun!"

"I will. See ya."

I leave the room and go downstairs, my boots tapping on the stairs as I go. I make my way through the kitchen and outside. The men and women are around a large table. I search for Viper and see him off to the side talking to another woman. She's attractive, petite with blonde hair.

She reaches for Viper, but he pulls away, shaking his head at her. *Hmm… past lover maybe.* He sees me and smiles, then swaggers over, leaving the woman. I inch to the side to see her mouth pinch as she stares at me with narrowed eyes, so I smile back at her. I'm used to modeling—and plenty of bitchiness. She's going to have to do a lot better than giving me the stink eye if she's trying to be intimidating.

Viper's arm comes around my shoulders and he pulls me to his side. "Ready to eat?"

A gigantic black dog strolls toward me. I leap up onto Viper's back and scream. He laughs, but I hang on for dear life.

"Conan," Ava calls.

The dog stops, then looks at Ava and trots back to her, which allows me to breathe again. When the dog is far enough away, I untangle my limbs from Viper's hard body and slide down until my feet meet the ground.

We make our way to the table, everyone staring at us. I still warily eye the dog. A few of the women stand. "Have our seats," a woman with black hair and tattoos on her arms says. "We're going to clear everyone else's plates."

I give her a small smile in appreciation.

"I'm Trixie."

A woman with glamorous makeup walks over to us. She nods in greeting. "I'm Mercedez."

"I'm Dolly," a woman with pink hair calls out from the other side of the table.

I shift, glancing back at the woman who looks like she wants to shiv me. "And you are?"

"Candy," she replies in a rather passive-aggressive tone.

My eyes flit from one woman to the next as I say, "I'm Sophie. It's a pleasure to meet all of you."

Candy storms off. Viper sighs.

"You don't owe her shit," says one of the men. It's Axle,

Elena's partner. With his larger-than-life personality, he's someone I couldn't forget. When my eyes land on Elena, she smiles at me across the table.

I make my way around the table to Zara and Knox. They both stand. I wrap my arms around Zara and squeeze. "Hello, gorgeous," I say to her.

She giggles and inches back. "I'm happy you decided to stay. I'm looking forward to spending time with you."

Lightness fills my chest. "I know, right? It's long overdue. We haven't spent much quality time together while I've been back here." I peek at the back door, which Candy went into after she left. "It should be interesting."

I move to Knox and give him a kiss on the cheek. "Good to see you."

"You too," he replies. He's never been a man of many words.

I walk back over and take a seat next to Viper. I lean into him, lowering my voice. "If you need to talk to Candy to get whatever it is between you sorted... I don't mind."

He inches back and his eyes widen. He takes a moment to answer. "Are you sure?"

I hardly know the guy, but I know that while I'm staying, I'm here for a good time. "Yep, go... it's fine."

He intently searches my eyes, then nods, but leans in, kisses my forehead, and whispers, "Thanks, wifey."

My heart beats a little too fast.

"There's lasagna, salad, and garlic bread," Ava says.

"I'll have salad."

"I can heat the lasagna and garlic bread up for you?" she asks softly.

"No, I'll just have the salad, but thank you."

She frowns. "I can cook you something else?"

I smile at her, remembering the way she kept apologizing to people on the dance floor in Vegas, such a darling. "I'm a health nut. If there's fruit inside, I'll grab a piece if I get hungry."

"There's plenty of fruit inside, in the bowl on the kitchen counter, and there's some in the fridge."

I lean over, grab a plate, and start piling salad on it.

"Did Viper go after Candy?" Axle asks.

I stab my fork in the salad. "Yes, he did."

Axle shakes his head.

"Do you remember everyone, or would you like me to introduce you to everyone?" Knox asks.

I leisurely glance around while chewing. Piper would have a field day. Every one of the men here is sexy in his own way. "I remember Reaper." Despite being a towering six-five, there's a softness in his eyes. My eyes dart around the table again. "Obviously, Elena and Ava and Axle. After that my mind is blurry."

There are chuckles around the table. "You were very drunk," Zara adds.

I lift my hand, displaying my wedding ring. "So drunk I got married," I say mockingly. Amusement shows on every-one's faces.

Bomber points to the guy next to him. "That's Demon." I gaze at him, taking in every inch of his ink-covered skin under his shirt and cut. "Twitch." The guy has thick, wavy hair and a pierced ear. He was sitting at the fire when I came back to get Viper to sign the divorce papers.

My eyes shift to Axle next, who has the same mischievous glint in his eyes that Viper does.

"The next man after Axle is Cash." He has short black hair and a light beard; he gives me a nod. Knox points to the last man. Well… young man. He was the other one by the fire. "And Rage." Rage gives me a shy smile, and I don't miss the slight pink on his cheeks. He's the only one not sporting a beard—he's clean-shaven.

"Thank you for having me."

"You never know… you could end up staying and living here," Axle mentions offhandedly.

I snort. "Not going to happen."

Viper takes a seat next to me. "Sorry," he says through a heavy breath.

"There's nothing to be sorry for," Axle pipes up. "We need to speak to the sweet butts. We don't want a repeat of last time with Vera and Grace."

I almost choke on a piece of food. "Sweet what?"

"Sweet butts," Axle says slowly. "Every other woman who lives here that isn't the wife or ol' lady of a patched member."

"The biker terms are going over my head. What happened last time?" I ask eagerly, intrigued by the biker gossip.

"They were bitches to Ava and Elena, so we kicked them out," Axle says.

"They weren't nice at all…" Ava utters, frowning.

"Jealousy, I gather?"

Ava nods.

"Don't worry about me, I can handle myself."

"You shouldn't have to," Reaper replies to me. That's sweet of him to say.

"I'll speak to them," Viper says.

Axle laughs. "Yeah, you seem to be doing a real good job so far." Viper picks a piece of garlic bread off his plate and throws it across the table, hitting Axle in the chest. "Hey!" Axle exclaims.

"I'll do it," Knox says. "I'll set Candy straight."

I mouth "thank you" at him across the table, and he gives me a tight nod. Gotta love my cousin. Knox, or Bomber, as they call him, has turned into such a handsome man. Sporting a more rugged appearance, his beard is longer and wilder compared to the others. When we were younger, he used to be more reserved, but now he carries a noticeable hardness.

Demon, the tattooed guy next to him, looks rough around the edges too.

I lift a tomato to my mouth and listen to the chatter amongst the group. The men seem decent… All the women but Candy seem friendly. I get to spend time with Zara and Knox. I think I'm going to enjoy spending time here, and after a month, I'm going back to New York… back to reality.

"There's a truck out front of our gates," Twitch says, then looks up from his phone. "Did someone order something?"

"Yes, the order's for me." *The new bed has arrived!*

After dinner, I grab my skincare bag and towel and make my way to the bathroom, where I lock the door behind me. I can't stop myself from checking the sink and then the shower, but to my surprise, everything looks clean. I blow out a breath—one less thing I have to worry about.

Following my shower, I wrap my fluffy towel around me. I line up my skincare products from first to last and apply them to my face and neck, then brush my teeth. When I'm finished, I return to the bedroom, where Viper is lying under the duvet, leaning back on his elbows.

"I was going to break in to check if you were still alive."

"Smartass!" I utter under my breath, but then I open my skincare product bag up wide. "It takes a long time to apply all of these."

His eyes widen. "Why do you need so many products?"

"Looking after my skin is important."

He frowns. "You don't need it."

"Oh, yes, I do. Do you even wear sunscreen?" I ask him.

"No."

I click my tongue. "You should. It will reduce wrinkles."

He just shakes his head at me, then a slow grin curves his lips. "I have to admit, these soft sheets and pillows are pretty comfy. The bed is the perfect firmness. Good choice!"

"I told you," I reply, amused.

I walk over to my suitcase and pull out my silk nightgown and thong, then drop the towel while smiling to myself. He clears his throat from behind me and my smile curves further. I'm not ashamed of my body, and it's nothing he hasn't seen before.

I step into my thong and deliberately, slowly pull it up my legs. I bring the nightgown over my head and let the silk fall and flutter over my skin.

"That was one of those most erotic things I've ever seen." His voice is deep and raspy.

I turn to him. He's staring at me with a predatory gaze. I step over to the bed and lie down. My body sinks into the mattress. I'm ready to jump his bones, but knowing I can't bolt in the morning and never see him again has me pausing. He never said I had to have sex with him as part of the deal, but I know I'll be lucky to last a week, let alone a month, without sex.

He shifts over to me. Once his body is flush against mine, I turn my back to him and back my ass further into his groin. I receive a growl in response. He pulls me closer until his hard dick is pressing against my ass.

I press my lips together to suppress a moan. I'm wet and ready, but today has been exhausting. He lifts his head and presses a kiss on my neck, then my shoulder, making me shiver.

"Night, Viper."

He doesn't complain, instead pulls me further into him.

"Night, wifey."

SIX

CHOKING ON JEALOUSY

Viper

My alarm rings, but I don't want to move, as I've woken up with a raging hard-on. "What's your alarm set for?" my little temptress asks.

Damn! I pry myself away from her and roll over. I snatch up my phone and turn off the alarm.

"Me and Rage go for a run," I say as I shuffle off the bed and adjust myself.

She sits up while I make my way to my wardrobe and pull out the drawer to grab a pair of shorts.

"I'm coming!" she says.

I smile. I'm going to enjoy watching her run.

Sophie's out of bed and bent over her suitcase. Her short nightdress has lifted, showing the edge of her ass, which makes me curse. This isn't helping my dick at all, so I turn away, pull out a War Brothers MC shirt, and pull it over my head. As much as I want to admire her body, I need to settle the fuck down. "I'll meet you downstairs," I tell her over my shoulder as I leave the room.

When I get downstairs, Rage is sitting at the dining table waiting for me. "Are you ready?" he asks.

I shake my head. "We're waiting on my wife."

His brows lift high. "Sophie's coming?"

"Apparently."

He chuckles. "How long is she going to take?"

I shrug. "Let's just hope she doesn't have to apply her twenty-step skincare routine to her face."

His head tilts. "Her what?"

"Don't worry… I hope not too long. She looked like she was getting changed as I was leaving the room."

"Do we go slow today or…?"

"How about we just match her pace," I answer.

"I'm ready." Sophie is jogging down the stairs. I greedily devour her body as she ties her long blonde hair up. She's wearing short black shorts with a white strip down each side that show every curve, like her luscious hips and those long lean legs. She's wearing a matching black sports bra, which has a matching white stripe around the under-boob band.

When Sophie reaches us, there's a teasing smile at the corner of her lips. I slowly circle her but stop when I see the shorts cup each cheek of her ass. "What are these?" I pull the material out of her ass, and when I let go it flings back into place. They're fucking hot and show off the curves of her delicious ass.

"Scrunch-bum shorts," she says matter-of-factly.

I look up to see Rage's head inching to the side as he tries to get a peek—not that I can blame him.

I throw my arms around her, enjoying the shriek that comes out of her mouth. Bringing my face into the crook of her neck, I say, "Temptress… you're killing me."

She laughs. "I thought I was wifey."

I let go of her, then grab her hand and swing her around to me. "You are both." The wicked glint in her eyes has me wondering how long it'll be before we have sex.

After I put my sneakers on, we walk out the front door to see the sun rising. As we move across the driveway, I wet my lips, bringing my thumb and index finger together and to my mouth. I whistle, and it only takes a moment before Conan is running full speed toward us.

Sophie lets out a shrill scream and darts behind me. I turn around to face her. "He won't hurt you."

She nods slowly, though her lips are pressed together. I grasp her hand in mine, linking our fingers together, and squeeze. When Conan doesn't acknowledge us, her shoulders loosen a bit. Conan darts past us and eagerly bounces around by the front gate, waiting for our morning run.

Rage opens the gate.

"Did you want to go for a walk or a jog?" I ask Sophie.

"A jog," she says in a clipped tone, like I just offended her for offering to go for a walk instead.

I can't stop my stupid grin. "No need to bite my dick off."

She laughs. We stride forward at a slow pace at first. Conan is ahead of us, zigzagging on the dirt path, his nose down as he sniffs around.

We jog over uneven ground. The dirt path is from tire tracks that lead up to a cabin, and further along is where we grow pot. "You go first," I tell Rage, so he can lead and I can feast on Sophie's body.

As Rage moves ahead of me, my eyes go straight to Sophie's breasts, which bounce with every stride, then to those mile-long legs, and all I can think is I can't wait to have her legs wrapped around my hips. I reluctantly force my eyes ahead of me. I need to stop it before I have another hard-on—that's going to be uncomfortable while running.

"Conan," I yell out when I can't see him up ahead. I can't

lose that dog; Ava will be devastated. He comes out of the long grass along the track and pauses, peeping back at us. "Wait there, shithead!" I hear Rage chuckle ahead of me.

As we jog further along up the hill, my blood is pumping, my heart is racing, and my breath is heavier. Apart from the early chirps of the birds, all I can hear is our footsteps hitting the ground and our heavy breathing. I dare a peek at Sophie again, surprised that she's keeping up with us. A light sheen of sweat covers her forehead and chest, making my mouth water. The sharp breaths through those plump lips of hers…

"Have you gotten a good look?" Sophie asks. Her honesty and saying what she's thinking is refreshing.

"Oh, wifey," I say through a smile. "I could stare at you all day and never get enough."

She shakes her head at me, though the corner of her mouth teases a smile.

We run in smooth, quick strides further up the hill, past the cabin, but as we get closer to where we grow our marijuana, I say, "How about we turn back? I'm starved." It's taken us twenty minutes to get to this point—that should be enough.

Rage stops, then turns, gives me a stiff nod, and jogs past me. We make our way back down the hill. As we get back to the clubhouse and our jog slows down to a walk, I wipe the sweat off my forehead with my forearm. When we get closer, the smell of bacon hits me. I wave Sophie over. "Come on, it smells like they're out back at the barbecue."

Her nose crinkles. "No, thanks."

A fatty meal after a run… I understand if she doesn't feel like it. "What would you like then?"

"Um… a smoothie or even some fruit."

"I can do that," I answer as we go inside. Rage goes to the side of the clubhouse, toward the barbecue.

As we walk through the house, Sophie asks, "What's in those rooms?"

I stop to see what she's looking at. "The first one is the computer and security room, and the one with the War Brothers MC logo carved into the door is church."

She blinks a few times. "What's church?"

"Where the club meetings are held."

We continue toward the kitchen, but she stops at the wall full of the MC's police mug shots, while I keep walking. Trixie and Candy are standing by the oven. Candy's face brightens when her eyes land on me. She takes two steps toward me but stops when she sees Sophie behind me. Candy's face falls. I need to keep reminding myself that she's not my problem.

"Mornin'," I say to the women in an upbeat voice.

Trixie smiles. "Good morning. How was your run?"

I wait a moment, giving Candy time to reply to me, but she looks away, grabs plates, and walks out the back door. *Unbelievable*. I turn my attention back to Trixie. "The scenery was much better this morning," I say as I peer at Sophie, who takes a seat at the counter.

Trixie grins, giving Sophie the once-over. "I bet it was…" Then she lowers her voice. "She's hot."

"Hi, Sophie," Trixie says, and Sophie replies, "Hey, Trixie."

I make my way to the cupboard and pull out the blender, set it on the counter, and then slide out a cutting board. "I'm putting vanilla protein powder in my smoothie."

She nods. "I'll have that too."

I shift my gaze to the fruit bowl. "And bananas."

"Sounds good," Sophie replies.

As I'm cutting the banana and putting the pieces in the blender, I think how good it is that we both enjoy exercise and eating clean.

After I blitz the smoothie, I pour the creamy liquid into a

glass and set it in front of her. She takes a sip. "Do you have a gym here?"

"Not here, though it's on our to-do list. There's one in Crown Village that me and some of the men go to a couple of days a week."

"Are you talking about the smaller one that's in the Crown Resort?"

I shake my head. "There's a newer one now. Do you know the Monroe and De Santis families?"

"Yes."

"Well, it's their youngest children, Mia and Ashton, who own it, though they're not children anymore."

Sophie looks thoughtful. "I want to go with you next time."

I won't say no if I get to see her in an outfit like that again. "Sure," I say, dragging out the word.

"Can we go on the motorcycle?" Sophie asks.

"Hell yeah," I reply. I can't wait.

Axle walks in through the back door, and when his eyes land on me, he beams. "My man... we're having a party for you two tonight." His gaze darts between me and Sophie.

"Oh yeah," I reply. "For what?"

"Your wedding—we haven't celebrated it yet."

Sophie coughs, like she just choked on her drink.

"Great. I can go to the store today; I wouldn't mind getting some more food."

Axle rolls his eyes at me. "Ava was going to do a baked dinner because she thought you two would like something healthy."

"That's thoughtful of her," Sophie replies.

"Get Ava to get a list together. We can go today," I tell Axle.

AFTER OUR SHOWERS, WE GET IN THE TRUCK AND DRIVE TO THE stores. We don't even get to the front door of the grocery store before a woman stops me in my stride. "Viper," she says, seductively. I've slept with her, but I can't remember her name. Her hand comes out to touch my cut until Sophie clears her throat from beside us and links our hands together, giving me a feisty smile. I wasn't expecting that, but Sophie's jealousy is a real turn-on.

The woman drops her hand, giving Sophie the once-over, and takes a step back. "So, it's true?" the woman says to me. "You're married?"

"Yes, he is," Sophie replies for me.

The woman purses her lips, nods, and walks away.

As we move inside and grab a shopping cart, Sophie asks, "How many of your side chicks shall we be running into today?"

I slowly shrug, though inside I'm cringing. After getting fruit, vegetables, yogurt, and a bunch of other healthy food for Sophie, me, and the club, we pay and then go to the liquor store next door.

We walk through the aisles, and Sophie places a couple of bottles of vodka in the cart.

"Thirsty?" I tease.

"It's for the shots," she answers. "And there's a lot of people that live at the clubhouse."

"What ones are you making?"

"Wet pussy…" she replies, and I laugh.

"We all loved that one."

"I bet. I'm getting ingredients for a few. I thought the jam donut and red-headed slut would be good too."

My brows lift high at the last name, though I guess she

would know what tastes the best, as she owns a club. I can tell it's going to be a good night.

We end up running into only two women who I've slept with, which I think is pretty good. After we get home, I help Rage put the liquor away behind the bar and then grab a drink and take a seat on the stool at the bar. Most of the women have gotten ready and are in the kitchen, helping Ava cook. Sophie still isn't down yet.

My insides are vibrating. I need to tie her ass down to my bed so that she can't leave and has to stay with me forever. I'm pretty sure I have handcuffs in there somewhere. I chuckle at the thought.

The men quieten, and Rage's eyes widen and his mouth falls open. Axle peers over my shoulder and then quickly looks away. I turn to see Sophie walking toward me in what has to be the world's shortest purple dress.

It's fitted and tight, hugs her curves, and shows off her flat stomach. She twirls with a flirty smile. A burning sensation sears through me, and I jolt to my feet. I pick her up and throw her over my shoulder. She squeals. I smack her firm ass as she wallops my back. "Viper!" she yells, though she doesn't sound serious whatsoever. I smack her again as I walk up the stairs.

I throw her on my bed when we get into the room, and she bounces from the impact. "Temptress, you look sexy as fuck, but you're not leaving this room until you have a longer dress on."

Her eyes narrow and she stands, squaring her shoulders. "Get over yourself. I'll wear what I want. No man tells me what to do."

"I'm not your average man. If you move an inch, everyone will see your sweet little pussy, and no one gets to see that but me."

She searches my eyes as if to see how serious I am, so I

turn and step back over to the door, close it behind me, and lean against it. "Don't believe me?" I ask, raising a brow. "Try me. We can stay in here all night… though as the celebration is about us, everyone is going to be disappointed if we don't attend."

Her jaw clenches. I cross my arms over my chest and yawn. If she thinks this is a negotiation, she has another thing coming.

She lets out a heavy breath and goes to her suitcase. My chest loosens. But the blue dress she picks out seems to be the same size, though with longer sleeves. "Are you kidding me?" I ask her. "It needs to be longer, covering more of your legs."

"I don't think I have any longer dresses here!"

"Hmm… shame you're going to miss the party then."

Her lethal stare is aimed at me. "What am I supposed to wear then?"

"Jeans it is."

"Jeans for a party?" Her nose crinkles. From the disturbed look on her face, anyone would think I was making her wear a knitted sweater.

"Correct." I look at my phone. "Time's tickin'." She pulls the dress over her head and throws it on the ground with more force than necessary. As she bends over, I see her sexy round ass in a white thong, and my dick wants out of my pants. I hold myself back from going to her. The only other thing that would seem more appealing on her ass is my handprint.

She effortlessly wriggles into a pair of white jeans and slips on a tight top that exposes her belly. "See, temptress… you look just as sexy." And… I can finally breathe.

She gives me a smile that says, "fuck you". A phone rings. It's not mine, and when I glance back to the bed, it's not hers either. It's coming from her suitcase. "Whose phone is that?" I ask her.

She waves me off. "My other phone."

"How many do you have?"

"Two."

"Then why do you need that one as well?" I say as I peer down at her suitcase.

As her slow sassy-ass smile grows, I have a sense I'm not going to like what she's going to say.

"It's my dick phone."

My mouth opens and I stare at her. "What... the... fuck is a dick phone?"

"The number I give out when I want dick." She answers so innocently that it contrasts with what she's actually saying. I stride to her. "What are you doing?" she asks. I bend, sifting through her clothes. "Hey!" she yelps.

The phone stops but then rings again. "Desperate asshole!" I mutter under my breath. I open the front zipper, pull the phone out, and answer it. "She's married now!" I hang up.

She tries to grab the phone back, but I turn, giving her my back, moving my arms out of her grasp as I pull the back off the phone and take out the SIM card. I snap the SIM card in half, turn, and place the pieces in her hands while slipping the phone into my back pocket.

She gasps. Usually, I couldn't give two fucks who women have or are sleeping with. I've always lived in the now, never, not once, focused on the future.

"Sorry, wifey, my dick's the *only* one you'll be riding for the next month." A thought comes to mind. I've seen the way she looks at me. If she's used to regular sex and wants me, then I can use it to my advantage. I smile at myself. I'm a genius.

SEVEN

SURRENDER AND COCKBLOCKING

Sophie

"I heard you got made to change," Zara points out in an amused voice.

I glare at Viper, who's playing pool across the room with Rage, Cash, and Candy, before directing my gaze back at Zara, who's sipping on the whiskey and cola I made for her.

"Hmm…" I mumble, half-annoyed that I crumbled but secretly loving being manhandled. Seeing the dominant side of him stirred something within me.

My lips pinch before I say, "He'd better not get used to winning."

"Winning?"

"He won by me giving in. That won't happen again." Unless I want it to.

She tilts her head to the side and squints. I sigh. "Don't worry about it," I answer. My cousin Knox is infatuated with her. She wouldn't know what playing games was.

"I'm not used to men standing up to me. This whole

spending night and day with the same person is clearly affecting me," I say as I twirl a finger next to my temple. "To my surprise, I liked it. Usually, I'd be mortified, but a fine man like him giving me an ultimatum hit differently." I think back to him standing by the door, his arms crossed, biceps bulging, and face stern, his voice deep and commanding… *Yum.* "I tell you what, though…" I say softly. "I don't think I'll be able to hold off on sex any longer."

She laughs, but I'm serious. I'm dying to have his hands on me again.

"How long have you lasted without sex?" she asks, curious.

"Over the last few years? Maybe five days."

"Five days?" she says in a high-pitched voice. "That's all… five days?"

"And it was one of the toughest times of my life," I say dramatically.

She smiles. "I've missed your sense of humor. I'm glad you're staying with us."

"Aw… I've missed you too."

I peer down at the shot glasses I've placed in front of me on the bar. "How many people are there?" I ask while counting the shot glasses. Zara looks off. "Sixteen, I think."

"This is going to take me a while." The shaker holds only four shots at a time.

"It's your party, I'll do it."

I shoo her away with my hand. "I'm happy to, and it's only a quiet celebration here at the MC."

After I finish, the music from outside gets louder. It's heavier music than I'm used to. "Can I change the music?"

Zara nods. "Ask Twitch. I think his phone is connected via Bluetooth."

"Sooo… Tell me a bit about the MC." I can't help myself from snooping.

"Uh… I don't know what to tell you. They got together after they finished in the military and formed, like, a brotherhood, I guess you could say. They help me with the women and children's shelter, which I'm so grateful for. I couldn't have met a better group of people."

"What else do they do?" I know they need to bring in money from somewhere. Zara averts her eyes. My gut is telling me it's something shady. "Zara," I say, with a pointed look. "What else do they do?"

She flinches. "Sorry, I thought you would know because of your family… but I can't say anything. I promised Bomber."

My body tenses. *Fabulous…* My family and the MC are in business together. If Zara won't tell me, I presume it's illegal. Annoyance and curiosity swirl through me. I make a mental note to ask Lawson what she's talking about.

"How's your club doing?" she asks.

I smile when I think of my achievement. "It's making a hell of a lot of money, so it's doing really well."

"Is it, like, a regular nightclub or…?"

"It's a medium-sized venue with different dancers every Friday and Saturday night, and we book in popular DJs. It's a modern vibe. Upstairs is VIP. You need to come and visit."

Her eyes brighten. "I will. It sounds great."

I point to Zara's vest, which I've noticed all the women who are in relationships have. "What's that?"

"A War Brothers MC property vest—it's like an engagement ring for bikers, but also a deterrent for other men when we are outside the clubhouse to say I'm with Bomber."

"Well… I'm married… so where's mine?"

She laughs. "Ask Viper for one. Cash usually orders them."

"Are these for me?" a teasing voice asks. I peer up to see Axle walking toward us, his eyes following along the line of shots.

"One shot is for you," I clarify. Knox walks in behind him. "I guess I should call you Bomber now," I say to my cousin. It's odd, but everyone except Zara calls him Bomber.

"Shots!" Axle yells over the music.

Everybody files in and stands around the bar. I don't miss Candy scurrying behind Viper. He gives me one of his sexy smiles. I know he's not into Candy that way… but I can't help the distaste that woman leaves in my mouth. "Where's my property patch, hmm?" I ask, giving Viper a playful scowl. They are badass. I want one.

Viper walks to me with open arms. "Does that mean you're staying with me after the bet is finished?"

I snort. "No."

He shrugs. "Guess you're not getting one then."

My eyes narrow at him then flick to Cash. "Can you order me one?"

Cash puts his hands up and backs away a step. "Don't bring me into the middle of this." Viper chuckles, the smartass.

Everyone grabs a full shot glass and holds it high. "To Sophie and Viper," Bomber says, then looks at me. "Welcome to the War Brothers MC family."

Everyone chants, "To Sophie and Viper." We clink glasses, and I down the shot, feeling both the burn and the sweetness of the peach schnapps.

The men slam their glasses on the bar counter. "I love me some wet pussaayyyssss," Axle says with a lopsided grin. He laughs when Elena rolls her eyes at him.

I notice Ava didn't take a shot. As the men walk away, I ask her, "Do you want something else?"

"No, thank you, I haven't been feeling well."

I frown. "What about a mocktail? I can make you a drink because we got some more fruit juice when we went shopping."

Her lips curve. "That I will say yes to."

"What do you feel like? I can make something tropical."

"That sounds good, thank you."

I make my way over to the kitchen while Ava, Elena, and Zara follow behind. They take a seat at the kitchen island while I pull out the blender. "Does anyone else want a mocktail or cocktail?"

Zara and Elena nod and smile. I get to work making a pineapple crush mocktail for Ava and a cocktail for Elena and Zara with pineapple, coconut water, lime, and the added shots. I can't believe we're having a so-called getting hitched celebration. Even though it's phony, I love me a party.

THE DRINKS ARE FLOWING, MY TECHNO MUSIC IS THUMPING, AND Zara, Ava, Elena, and I are sitting outside by the fire, talking and laughing. My body is toasty warm from the fire. Its flames are high, sending sparks into the night sky.

"I still can't believe you're with Viper," Elena says next to me. "Axle told me Viper was the manwhore of the club, and at the beginning, I saw him hook up with different women during parties and stuff, but then Candy got her hooks into him. He calmed down a little, but as soon as there were other chicks here for parties, he would be with them instead."

"What's Candy's deal? If he has been with others, I'm obviously not the first."

"Viper always seemed unattainable," Elena replies. "His flirty attitude suggested he was up for a good time, never anything serious, but he married you… It's a big deal with a commitment-phobe like him, which makes me think Candy's jealous that she never got that part of him."

"What's Candy like?" I ask them. "I'm getting the impression she's not too happy with me being here."

Elena nods. "She's usually bubbly and happy, but I've noticed a change in her since you've been here. The jealousy is clear—she's either glaring or frowning at you."

Ava moves forward an inch so I can see her clearly, as she's sitting on the other side of Elena. "I agree. Candy's been sweet since I've been here, but I guess there's this different side of her we've never seen before."

"How's your stay been? Is it better than you imagined?" Zara asks me.

I stare into the fire, taking a sip of my cocktail before answering. "It's surprised me, actually. I can still be in my routine, and it makes it easier that Viper shares the same interests. Like partying"—I raise my glass—"and exercising. I'm just waiting for my laptop so that I can keep on top of managing my business, and I'm going for a motorcycle ride tomorrow."

Zara puts her hand on my arm. "Oh… you're going to love the ride. It's so much fun."

"So much fun…" Elena agrees. "There's nothing quite like it."

I smile. I can't wait.

Viper, Reaper, Bomber, Demon, and Axle are at one end of the table, smoking cigars. Some of the single guys—Twitch, Rage, and Cash—are at the other end with Mercedez, Trixie, and Dolly, playing strip poker. It's amusing, as Mercedez and Dolly are playing while trying to cover their boobs and hold the cards at the same time. Trixie has only lost her top, while Twitch and Cash are fully clothed and Rage is sitting there naked. God, that young man has a delicious body, with his carved-out eight-pack of defined muscle and tanned skin. If I was younger and not with Viper, I would go after him.

Twitch places all his cards on the table with a large, smug

grin. The women smile, apart from Trixie, who yells, "Cheater!"

Twitch replies, "Sore loser," while Cash and Rage laugh.

Sitting next to the women is Candy, her eyes darting from the game to Viper. Then she moves and takes a seat next to him. I glare as her hand goes to his lap. Though it looks like he's not giving her any attention and is talking to the men, it still irritates me.

"Excuse me, blondie!" I yell out. Candy and Viper glance in my direction. "Hands off my husband!" I say as I give her hand on Viper's leg a pointed look. She swiftly moves her hand as Viper's lips curve up into a smirk.

Since I've made Twitch change the Bluetooth from his to my songs, I go to my playlist, browse through, and choose an old song—"Hello" by Stafford Brothers, Lil Wayne, and Christina Milian—and turn it up. I place my drink on the ground and then stand. The women smile broadly as I shake my hips from left to right, in line with the beat.

I wave them up, and the three of them stand. I grab Zara's hand, and we effortlessly sashay our hips to the rhythm. I drop low in a seductive move, then spring back up. Zara laughs and looks over my shoulder but then lets go of my hand, so I turn. Viper grabs my hand instead, catching me around the waist and spinning us, making me smile.

As I surrender to his lead, he moves behind me, rubbing himself up against me to the beat. The desire between us sets my skin on fire as my cheeks heat and yearning flares, shooting to every nerve ending in my body. His hands wander over my hips and under my shirt to rest on my bare stomach. He sways behind me, bending his knees, aligning his body with mine. I close my eyes, losing myself to the music.

Our dirty dancing is exhilarating, and I'm getting high as I grind my ass into the crotch of his pants. I hear a wolf whistle and laughs over the music, but I seductively intertwine our bodies, blocking them out.

When a new track plays, he spins me out, then brings me back to face him. The lust in Viper's eyes sends a shiver rocketing through me. My eyes lower to his lips, and I run my tongue over mine in anticipation. My arms circle his shoulders. I pull his head toward me and take his lips with mine. Our lips caress each other passionately, our tongues plunging deep.

I run my fingers through his styled hair, lost in him, wishing he hadn't made me change. The denim we're both wearing is too thick. I'm giddy with booze and eagerness. His hands firmly cup my ass as his eyes dance with greed. He yanks me higher, lifting my feet off the ground. I wrap my legs around his waist.

The night seems to get hotter; my skin is sheened with light perspiration. "Bed. Now!" he says through heavy breaths.

I'm panting… though I don't know if I can wait that long. My legs leave his hips, and as soon as my feet touch the ground, I grab his hand and pull him toward the side of the house, but he pulls me away toward the back door.

"No fucking way are we doing it here."

No one would see us around the side of the house unless they went looking for us, which is highly unlikely, and I'm desperate.

I stride next to him, rushing inside and toward the stairs as the heat of my blood sears through my veins, my self-control leaving me with every step toward his door. Lust makes my lips reach for his as our bodies crash and stumble together through his bedroom door. We undo and kick off our jeans, then I lift my shirt over my head and we fall together on the bed, his body over mine.

He breaks the kiss to lift his shirt over his head. My hands slide over his broad shoulders to his defined pecs, and then slowly over each ab. I peek at his big thick dick and lick my lips. When I make eye contact, dark predatory eyes stare back at me. He catches my lips again as he roughly squeezes my breast, making me moan. His expert hands roll my hard, tender nipple, sending shockwaves to my core.

"Are you wet for me?" he asks in a husky voice.

"Soaking…" I tease.

He groans, then sits up, slipping his hand between my shamelessly open legs. His finger parts my lips and glides into me with ease. I'm aroused, my body feverish. I close my eyes to escape the vulnerability of this position.

"You're so tight," he says before he pulls out and thrusts back inside. I clench him greedily. He pushes in two fingers, making my back arch off the mattress, and thrusts in and out with a skilled touch. "You know I've been thinking of having you every second of every day since that night?"

"Hmm…" I mumble, entrenched in chasing my orgasm. Even though the night we spent together is hazy at best, I've been thinking of him, but I keep my lips mashed together, not wanting to give him the satisfaction I was thinking of him too.

"You're mine now," he says as the pad of his thumb circles my clit. Instead of turning me off with his macho bullshit, he only pushes me closer to orgasm as my core tightens and the tension builds.

"I want to see you when you come." My eyes squeeze shut. He lifts his thumb from my clit, making my eyes fly open. "Good girl," he purrs.

When his thumb returns to massaging my clit, I cry out, riding my orgasm as pleasure pulses through me. My body goes limp as I gradually come out of my daze. I smile up at him.

Gorgeous face—check.

Abs—check.

Big dick—check.

Sense of humor—check.

To hit the jackpot, I need to see if he *gives* good dick. I lean over, trying to grab him, but he pauses; then his head tilts, and something flashes across his face. "Oh yeah… I forgot," he says with a cocky look in his eyes.

"Forgot what? What are you waiting for?" I ask as impatience itches at me. I know I just got off, but I want him inside of me.

Instead, he stands, and my mouth falls open as he grabs his jeans and pulls them up. He cringes when he has to bring the jeans over his hips.

"What are you doing?" I ask. "I thought we were going to have sex?"

"I can't wait to fuck you… over and over again… but I've decided you're not getting my dick until you promise you'll stay with me past the month that you agreed to."

I square my shoulders. "You conniving… manipulative… evil man."

He laughs and then drags his shirt over his head, taking away my view of his hard, muscled body. "I want dick!" I yell angrily.

"Stay married to me then, and I'll give you as much cock as you can handle." The sweetness of his tone makes me want to throttle him.

"I can't believe you're cockblocking me!"

He laughs again.

"Then why bother getting undressed?" I demand.

"I only just remembered. Now you know what you're missing out on," he purrs. I pick a pillow up and throw it at him. He won't last long without sex with me… I'll make sure of it.

EIGHT
NEVER GOOD ENOUGH

I MADE VIPER SLEEP ON THE COUCH IN HIS OWN CLUBHOUSE. *Screw him!* The balls he's got to even think he could affect me… even though he does. It's outrageous! No one has ever denied me dick before… like, he's hurting both of us. It's been one whole day, and I've been slumming it, binging Netflix with Ava, Elena, and Zara while the men are off doing whatever the fuck they do.

"Do you need any help with the charity?" I ask Zara. I'm bored and overthinking being denied sex. I might as well make myself useful.

"No, not really, but thanks for offering," she replies.

"If you're looking for something to do, you can help me cook for them," Ava offers, and that makes me laugh. She frowns.

"I can't cook," I clarify.

"Everyone can cook!" Ava says.

I shake my head. "Unless you want everyone throwing up afterward… then trust me… I can't cook."

"It's okay. I can't cook either," Elena chimes in.

"If anyone needs cocktails… that's something I can do."

I look to Zara. "Have you got enough people invested in the charity? Do you need money for anything?" Money is what I can offer.

Zara smiles. "Your family has already given us the hall for the charity to operate out of."

It's the least we could do. "We already owned it. It didn't cost us anything to give it to you, so tell me what you are lacking at the center… Do you want to extend it? I can contribute because Lawson and I were already talking about putting in money, and if we do, you know Alec and Harrison will. I don't want you to have to worry about anything. You tell us what you need, and it's done."

Zara's glassy eyes make me frown, and I lean over to hug her. "I love you, let us help you. It would be our honor to offer money for your charity to help the women and children. Honestly, I wish we had thought about it sooner."

She hastily brushes her eyes as more tears well up.

My phone rings. "Dad" pops up on my screen.

"Are you going to answer that?" Zara asks.

I roll my shoulders back, trying to ease my tension. "Oh… hell no."

She giggles. "Why?"

"Dad's calling for a specific reason, and I'm sure that reason has something to do with me randomly marrying a biker. I'm in my twenties… I don't need the lecture, and trust me, there will be a lecture. The main problem is that Viper's a biker, so Dad's going to be seeing red. I'll get the 'he's not good enough and only wants my money' speech. Business has always been Dad's strong suit… not family."

A deep frown curves on Ava's face. "That's really sad. Me

and Elena aren't close with our parents either, but since I've been here, family to me is everyone in the MC. Blood isn't everything."

Blood isn't everything… that echoes deep in my soul. "I have my brothers… Well, we were closer when growing up because we only had each other. Dad worked long hours, and Mom left us when I was young. I barely even remember her. After school, I moved to New York. My best friend, Piper, is the closest thing I've had to family."

I don't have many close people in my life, but I've always valued quality people over quantity. The abandonment issues I have from Mom and my fear of being rejected and undervalued by my father are why I've never wanted to get too close to a man. I have enough issues.

Now it's Zara wrapping her arms around me. I've missed having someone who knows my past and understands it. Piper is there for me, but she wasn't there with me growing up. Zara was, during the holidays when I returned home. She gets it.

"I'm here if you ever want to talk," she says softly.

I offer a warm smile. "Thanks."

"Weren't you going on a motorcycle ride?" Zara asks.

I tut. "Hmm… I was supposed to, but Viper pissed me off. Now I'm kind of annoyed at myself because I wish I could go to the gym to let some of my pent-up anger out."

"Oh…" Zara mutters. "What did he do?"

My arms cross my chest. The burn of annoyance still undeniably has its talons in me. "He's cockblocking me."

The women all laugh.

My eyes narrow. "It's not funny!"

"It kind of is," Zara replies while I pout. "Why is he cockblocking you?" she asks through giggles.

"He's using his dick against me!"

Elena holds her stomach as the women still laugh around me.

"He's trying to weasel his way in and get me to stay longer and not divorce his ass when the month is up. I can't even get it elsewhere because part of the deal is that we don't have"—I make air quotes—"sex or anything with anyone else."

Elena sighs. "My stomach hurts. That's so funny. What are you going to do?"

Suddenly I feel lighter, I smile mischievously. "He wants to play games, then karma is coming his way."

The dog barks outside, and after a couple of minutes, we hear talking at the front door and see Twitch walking toward us, a rectangular box in hand. "Is this yours?" he asks me.

I heave a sigh of relief and go to him, grasp the box, and pull it to my chest. "Oh… finally, my laptop." I peer back at Twitch. "Thank you!"

He nods and walks away. My eyes go straight to his behind. "He's hot." His jeans are baggy, but there's this undeniably chilled sexy vibe he has that's appealing.

Zara mashes her lips together as if hiding a smile.

After I open the box and pull my laptop out, my phone rings again, and it's Dad. He's nothing but persistent. I hurl the phone onto the couch and wail, "I need my ice cream, damn it!"

"You've got ice cream?" Elena asks.

I nod. "Ice cream… is my downfall. I eat healthy all the time, but when I'm stressed, ice cream is my comfort food. It's a small tub, so sorry… I can't share." Am I genuinely sorry? *Nope!*

I go to the kitchen, take out my cookie dough ice cream, grab a spoon, and make my way back over to the couch. No bowl is needed: I'll be a pig and eat it straight from the container. After opening the top, I take a big spoonful, and just as I'm about to bring it to my mouth, I hear, "What do we have here?" Twitch is standing behind me, looking at my ice cream.

"Watch him!" Elena says. "He has a sweet tooth."

"Twitch," I warn, "if you dare touch my ice cream, I'll smother you in your sleep."

He bursts out laughing and looks at Zara. "I like her!"

I lift the massive spoonful and enjoy the sweet taste of *my* ice cream. But afterward, my phone rings again, making me groan. I bite the bullet and answer it in a sickly sweet voice. "Hello, Dad."

"A biker, Sophie!" he yells, making me recoil. My mouth opens, then closes, then opens, but my tongue finds no words. "I had to hear from your brother that you're married. Imagine my surprise when I didn't get an invitation to *my daughter's wedding.*"

My pulse quickens as I stumble to find the right words. "I'm… uh…" Stupid Alec and his big mouth, though I bet he couldn't wait to tell Dad, damn brownnoser.

"I can't believe…" He breathes heavily. "Being the wife of a biker is dangerous. After all the years I've ensured your safety, you spit on that and marry the worst possible person. I raised you to be smarter than that."

His disapproval makes my stomach plummet. I knew he would be upset but… I didn't expect it to be this bad. "It was one night… a mistake," I say softly.

"It is a colossal fuckup! And no prenup… no contract… no nothing," he rages.

I swallow over the lump in my throat. "Well… don't worry about me. Viper's not interested in my money."

"How can I not worry about you when you make hasty decisions like that?" he says. His voice is losing its edge. "You can't tell me he wasn't aware of how wealthy you are. He's not husband material—he's a dangerous, money-hungry outlaw."

An uncomfortable feeling surges through me. Did Viper marry me because of money? I hate how Dad plants these negative seeds inside my head.

"Am I going to be meeting this *husband* of yours?"

"In a month," I answer, as the corner of my mouth twitches. All of it will be over with and we won't have anything to discuss apart from his disappointment in me.

"Today." His tone is non-negotiable.

I have the urge to disagree, but I hate arguing with him and don't want him showing up at the clubhouse causing trouble either. I should just get it over and done with… twenty minutes… in and out.

"Okay… we will see you today."

If Viper is desperate for me to stay married to him, I'll see if he feels the same after he meets my father. In turn, I might find out what my dad's connection is with the MC.

NINE

THE FATHER-IN-LAW
FROM HELL

Viper

After shooting practice, I walk inside to see Temptress and the other women sitting in the kitchen. I have to keep reminding myself that she needs to be savored. I need to use everything in my arsenal to convince her to stay. Even if that means holding out on sex. I just hope it pays off because I'm struggling already, but I must think of the long game. If she stays, I'll get to keep waking up to that beautiful face, rocking body, and shitload of sass.

"Are you free today?" Sophie asks.

My head tilts, and the side of my lip curves. "For you wifey, I'm free all the time."

Her fingers tap on the countertop. "Would you be ready to leave soon?"

I search her eyes; she's acting strange. "What are we doing? A motorcycle ride to the gym?" I struggle to contain my excitement.

"We have to visit my dad. He wants to meet you."

My buzz is obliterated… "I can't say I've ever met a woman's dad." I've never hung around long enough, but I'm charming… I'm sure I can navigate the meeting while proving I'm going to treat Sophie well and being careful not to cause any waves between our MC and her dad, Garrett.

The MC and her dad have a deal. We grow and sell large amounts of pot; her family allows us to do that with no interruptions from the police and safe travel through Crown Village and the surrounding towns. If her family was to turn against us, it could have very bad consequences for the MC.

"Oh, I can't wait," I say, sarcasm dripping from my words.

The women chuckle, while Sophie raises a perfectly manicured eyebrow and purses her lips. "Hmm… I bet." She glances down at the gym clothes she's wearing. "Well, I'll go get some clothes to wear to Dad's and we can get ready after the gym."

"Are we going out somewhere for dinner or something?" I don't understand why she has to get changed.

She shakes her head. Oh… it's for her father. Of course! "Ah, I hope you aren't expecting me to dress up."

She smiles. "I'm not."

I try to suppress my relief.

"Do you want me to grab you some gym clothes and a pair of shoes?" she asks.

"Yeah, thanks." Since I'm wearing my usual MC clothes.

After Sophie goes upstairs, I go in search of Bomber and find him in the hallway. "Tell me everything about your uncle Garrett."

He frowns. "Why?"

"Because me and Sophie are leaving within the hour to go to the gym, and then I have to meet her father."

His face tightens. "Don't fuck it up!"

"Can't you call and put a good word in for me?" Hope filters through my words.

He shakes his head. "It won't work… not with him… He doesn't like bikers. He only puts up with us because I'm his nephew and he gets a cut of the profits. It won't matter what I say about you—he'll just think you're a coward for getting someone else to put in a good word. He's old-school and big on respect, and just the fact that you didn't even meet him before marrying her, he's going to be uptight about."

I run a hand through my hair. "What will score me points with him?"

"Nothing… Sophie's his only daughter. He's always been overprotective of her, and you're an outlaw, so he's already going to hate the idea you two are together. He's not the type of person you can manipulate—he'll see right through it. Gifts won't work, and the only other things that matter to him are his family's businesses and his family's legacy, and you've kind of shit all over that."

My head falls back as I groan. "How come the only woman I've ever wanted is a Crown? What luck do I have that she's got Garrett as a father?" I cringe. "No offense…" Bomber is Sophie's cousin, after all.

"None taken. I don't envy you, that's for sure, but watch what you say to him."

I hear someone approaching. Temptress is walking down the stairs with a small bag on her back. I put my arm out, gesturing she should walk ahead of me. She's wearing those fucking ass-curving shorts again. I glance up at the ceiling. She's going to be the death of me.

My dick wants her… but I'm here for the long haul. Well… that's what I've got to keep reminding myself because holy smoke… all I want to do is haul her ass back into my room. My eyes devour every curve as we make our way through the clubhouse and outside.

Whack! I slap her ass… hard. She shrieks and jumps, then turns to me. I see the flash of excitement in her eyes before they narrow at me. I curse at myself… she's not making this easy for me… I'm not making this easy for me.

I grab the helmet that's hanging off Bomber's bike and hand it to her. "It's Zara's."

She frowns. "When do I get my own?" Before I can answer, she says, "And don't say only if I stay longer."

I nod, agreeing with her. "We'll get you a helmet today when we're out." She needs one for her safety, and from the way she's eyeing my bike, I'd say it's another thing on the list that she likes, which works in my favor. When she pulls the helmet on over her head, her long blonde braid hangs out at the back.

I swing my leg over my bike and hop on, grab my helmet and pull it over my head, and glance over at her. "C'mon wifey, it's your turn. Get on my bike and hold on to me." She slides onto the back of my motorcycle, wraps her arms around my waist, and leans into me. I smile. "Hold on tightly." After she tightens her hold, I start the engine, and we accelerate down the road. I enjoy the sensation of her body pressed up against mine.

When we arrive at the gym, I park and wait for her to climb off. Once I do too, she hands me the helmet. "I love it!" she beams.

I pull off my helmet and grin at her. "Good to hear it, wifey… good to hear."

When we walk through the gym's automatic doors, the cool AC hits me. Mia, the gym owner, greets us with a smile at reception.

"Mia, this is Sophie. She'll be casual here for the next month… or so." Sophie raises a brow.

"Nice to meet you, Sophie." Mia places paper and a pen in front of her. "Can you please fill this out and I'll grab you a casual pass?"

Sophie smiles back at her, then Mia leaves and Sophie

looks around at the gym. It has lines of ellipticals, treadmills, and bikes at the front of the room, with the machine equipment and weights in the middle and a boxing ring at the back.

"How old is this gym?" she asks.

"A few years now. Mia set it up with her boyfriend, Ashton."

She bobs her head. "Good on them. She looks young."

"About Rage's age."

Sophie fills out the paperwork, and Mia hands her a pass.

"Where's the locker rooms?" Sophie asks.

We swipe in, and I point toward them. We walk together, and when we reach the women's room, she takes the bag from her back, takes out my clothes and shoes, and passes them to me.

"I'll meet you back here."

"Okay," she replies, and I make my way to the men's room. After getting changed, I put my clothes in a locker and go out and stand by the door to the sauna, which is off to the side of the restrooms. When she walks out, I say, "I think you should stop wearing those shorts to the gym."

She huffs. "I think not."

There's an internal tug of war… I'm enjoying checking her out, but the thought of every other male in the gym perving on her… makes my blood boil.

Her eyes roam across me. I'm wearing a tank top with a deep V-neck that shows off my chest and arms. She licks her lips in approval. I press the door to the sauna, open it, and peek inside. No one is in there. I grasp her arm and pull her inside.

She giggles loudly. My hands go to her waist, and I squeeze firmly as her hands rise and rest on my chest. She lifts herself higher on her toes and whispers, "You could have me right now if you wanted." She runs a hand over my chest, my abs, and then grabs my dick through my shorts, making my heart thump and a shiver travel through me.

She rubs her hand up and down along my shaft, making me hiss. I keep eye contact because she's trying to get a rise out of me… trying to make me cave. I'm stubborn as fuck.

I find the strength to say, "Stay and be my wife… and I will." I try to keep my voice even.

She lets go and takes a step back. "No deal! Let's get going then."

I open the door and follow her out, then give her another smack on the ass for good measure.

"Viper!" She dares to reprimand me, after what she just did. *Unbelievable.*

"Are you going to behave today, or do I have to spank you again?"

She bats her eyelashes and draws a halo above her head with her finger.

"I'll take that as a no."

We move to the treadmills. I don't miss the way the men stop what they are doing and boldly stare at her, so I quicken my pace and walk close to her. Once they see me, their eyes dart away. Yeah, that's right, motherfuckers… she's mine.

I sense women's eyes on me, but my eyes never leave Sophie. My insides are vibrating at seeing Sophie in action. When two treadmills are free next to each other, she steps up to one, and I step over to the other and place my water bottle in the holder.

We power walk to warm up. Every time I increase my pace, she matches me. She's competitive, though I shouldn't be surprised. I hit my stride and go into a fast jog, and so does she. When I glance at her, she flashes me a grin. She's fit and puts the incline on, while I slow down. I'm itching to go to the weights, but I don't want her to get mauled by all the men either.

"Will you be alright if I go to the weights?"

Her eyes narrow and she raises her chin. "I'm a big girl. I don't need a big bad biker watching over me."

I dig her independence, so I make my way to the weight area.

After our workout, we get changed and leave on my motorcycle. We go to the bike shop first to get her a helmet. Then we ride to Sophie's family's home. My eyes bulge as we ride down the pebbled driveway to the three-story modern mansion. It's set on a cliff and overlooks the lake.

I park next to the Rolls-Royce, and when I get off my bike, I take my helmet off and gawk. "You have your own jetty too?"

Sophie lowers her eyes and gives me a tight nod.

"What's wrong?" I lift her chin to make eye contact. "We can leave now if you want."

Her eyes are flat. "This house doesn't have many good memories attached to it, apart from being with my brothers."

I raise my brow. "Didn't you grow up here?"

"Our mom took off when we were young. We never heard from her again, so Dad got full custody, but we were raised by nannies."

A heavy pressure takes root in my chest. "Did you ever want to find her?"

"I wanted to when I was young," she replies in a timid voice. "I was the only girl in between three brothers, and Dad was rarely there for us. I dreamed of Mom coming back… but she never did."

She pauses and shifts, looking out at the lake. "When me and my brothers were teenagers, we made a pact that we weren't going to search for our mom who didn't fight hard enough to see us." Sophie's head turns swiftly to me, her eyes wide. Her lips smack together as if she just shared something she didn't mean to.

I swallow as I imagine Sophie as a small child wanting her mother. I put my arms around her and bring her to my chest. She startles at first but then wraps her arms around me, snuggling in momentarily, before she pulls back and wipes her eyes, plastering one of her fake smiles on her face. I link my fingers in between hers. "Let's meet this father of yours."

She releases a shaky breath, which doesn't give me any confidence. We walk toward the front door, which has a guard standing beside it. I smile at the man, who's wearing a black suit and has a stern face. "Hey, man," I say to him. He doesn't answer or even crack a smile, just opens the door and greets Sophie. *Dick!*

We walk through the mansion. It's decorated with fancy furniture and fancy artwork, which makes me laugh inappropriately. This is like day and night compared to our clubhouse. Don't get me wrong, ours is nice, but this place… this place reeks of money.

We pass through the hallways and into a living room with floor-to-ceiling windows that look out on the lake. As I said… *fancy*… Garrett, dressed in a white collared shirt and black dress pants, stands tall. His body is rigid. Tension radiates off him in waves.

"Hey, Dad," Sophie says. She leans up and kisses his cheek, before giving him a brief hug. She turns to me. "This is Viper… I mean Brayden."

I hold out my hand. His scrutinizing eyes skim my face and then flick to my motorcycle vest. He shakes my hand with a firm, painful grip, though I don't show weakness. Instead, I paint on one of my charming smiles. "Nice to meet you."

"Can't say I feel the same." His harsh voice and the hatred in his eyes say this isn't going to be a friendly chat. Garrett is known as the cutthroat businessman who has police officers, judges, and other powerful people in his pocket.

"Have you two met?" Sophie asks, glancing between the two of us.

"No," Garrett answers her bluntly. He gestures toward the lounges, so we take a seat. He sits across from us. The awkward silence is deafening. Sophie crosses her legs, then uncrosses them.

Garrett peers at Sophie. "How's your business doing since you've been"—he glares at me—"*gallivanting* around."

She flinches, then clears her throat. "My focus is still on my business."

Garrett looks down at her hand where her wedding ring is and grunts. "It's clear that's not the case. Businesses don't run themselves. They require dedication, and it seems you've lost sight of that."

That was a low blow, but I see straight through Garrett. He's making her feel bad for being with me.

"She's managing her business from her laptop. Hell… I'm proud of her," I tell the dick. Sophie looks at me with a smile that lights up her beautiful face.

A sneer curves his lips. "In talking about careers, have you told your *wife* what you do?"

I sit up straighter. "It's club business… so no, I haven't told her. If you choose to tell her, that's your choice, but I can't."

Garrett's lips spread into a smile. His eyes dart back to Sophie. "They grow, distribute, and sell large quantities of marijuana."

"Oh, is that all…" Sophie responds, making some of the tension in my body loosen.

"I allow their cargo"—his head turns to me and his eyes narrow—"to have *safe passage* through Crown Village."

He wanted me here to remind his daughter that I'm not good enough and to threaten me at the same time. *Message received.*

"The MC also hosts illegal fighting and gambling," he's quick to point out.

I raise a brow at the self-satisfaction in his tone. Fuck this… and fuck him, so I add, "Then you also must know how the MC helps Misty's Safe Haven." We aren't the pieces of shit that he's suggesting we are. We do good too. His flinch and the twist of his face makes me inwardly smile.

His eyes cut to Sophie. "I can't believe you got married to a biker. I thought I brought you up better than that."

"Excuse me?" I ask. It's my turn to glare at him.

Sophie rests her hand on my leg. When I glance at her, she shakes her head at me.

I'm not shutting up. "Look, I came here to meet you for Sophie's sake. We got married. You can't change the past; it is what it is. And you don't need to tell me I'm not good enough for Sophie… I already know that." I peek at Sophie, whose face softens.

Garrett chuckles, but his laugh is deadly cold. "You just happen to marry the wealthiest woman you've ever met and expect me to what… bless the marriage?" He huffs. "It's the worst decision Sophie's ever made."

Sophie lets out a heavy sigh. I look at her closely. She's usually full of sass and comebacks.

"And don't even think you're getting a cent in the divorce."

Annoyance flares. "She can keep her money. I don't want it. It's not why I married her. She's motivated, hardworking, and successful. Hell, have a contract set up now that says I get nothing from her, and I'll sign it."

He chuckles again and slowly raises a brow. "I'll entertain the fact that you'll sign a contract. I'll have the contract to you by the end of the day."

He doesn't know me at all. "So… are we done?" I ask him, well and truly over this conversation.

Sophie stands to signal we are, so I stand with her. She leans down and kisses Garrett's cheek. "As always… pleasant chat, Dad," she says in a toneless voice.

When she walks away, Garrett rises to his full height and steps toward me. "I can't change the past, but I can change the future, and I will force your hand one way or another. If your club is caught in the crossfire, so be it."

My shoulders roll back and I glower at him. "You threatening *my* club?"

"You bet I am. She's family and deserves better"—he makes a point of looking me up and down, then scrunches his nose—"than what you could ever provide for her."

My hands clench by my side, but I force a smile. I have only so much patience. I turn my back to him and go outside.

I meet Sophie by my bike. Thanks to that asshole, I can't even enjoy my ride back to the clubhouse.

TEN

VIPER'S STUPID PERFECT BODY

Sophie

Once we get back to the clubhouse, Viper is quieter than normal, and it makes me think Dad's said something to him. I'm in my twenties… I don't need my father's approval, but it sucks I still crave it. Viper might be a biker, but he's not a terrible person. To think I verbal-diarrhead my childhood trauma makes me wince again.

He jogs down the stairs, taking them two at a time as he puts his earbuds in his ears. When he sees me, he says, "I'm going for a run."

"Again? We went to the gym this morning."

His gaze drops to the floor. "Yeah… I'll be back in an hour."

I frown but bob my head and then watch him leave the house. I make my way to the freezer and pull out my ice cream.

"Uh-oh… what's wrong?" Twitch asks, giving my ice cream a pointed stare.

I pull a spoon from the drawer. "I'm stressed out, that's what."

He laughs. "The meeting didn't go well, I take it."

I pull the lid off and scoop out a massive spoonful, ensuring that I get as much cookie dough as possible. "No, it did not. Where are the women?" I ask before I spoon the ice cream into my mouth, enjoying the sweet taste.

"Helping at the charity today."

I need a distraction. "So, are you and Mercedez a thing or...?"

With a small shake of his head, he says, "Nope... we just have sex."

I do like honesty. "Twitch, give me the goss... who is Trixie with, and what about Dolly?"

He blinks a few times at me. "Trixie and Dolly have sex with any one of the single men."

I take another spoonful as I pair everyone up. "What about Demon?"

"I was told he goes into the city for his needs."

I tilt my head as I suck on the spoon. "What needs does he have?"

A small smile tickles the edge of his lip. "You sure you want to hear this shit?" His warning tone suggests that I don't.

"Yes, I need a distraction... so go ahead... Demon goes to the city for..."

"He apparently goes to the sex club there."

I inch back. "Wow... I wasn't expecting that." Interesting though. "But why travel when there are women here?"

"He has particular *needs*..."

I'm torn between wanting to know and not wanting to know. "Well... he's committed, I'll give him that."

Axle walks into the kitchen and spots us. "Since when do

we have ice cream?" he asks while walking to the freezer. He opens it wide and moves things around.

"It's *my* ice cream," I reply.

"Yeah… I wouldn't touch her ice cream, man. She's already threatened me with death if I have any."

Axle closes the freezer and laughs, but when he looks at my face, his smile falls. "Oh… you're serious."

"You bet I am!"

"What were you two whispering about, anyway?" Axle asks us.

"I'm just finding out the MC goss."

"Oh well…" Axle wiggles his eyebrows. "Do fill me in."

I giggle. "Nothing you don't already know… like who likes who… who's sleeping with who…"

Axle's gaze whips to Twitch, and he grins evilly. Twitch's eyes tighten and he shakes his head at Axle.

My eyes bounce between them. "Whatever silent discussion is going on, I want to know about it."

Axle peers at me, that grin still firmly on his face. "Twitch has got a hard-on for Milly, Reaper's sister."

"I do not!" Twitch pipes up.

I lean toward them. "Do tell! Now I'm thoroughly invested."

Axle opens his mouth but chances a peek at Twitch and slams it shut. "Sorry… I can't."

I let out an exaggerated groan and then look at Twitch with pleading eyes.

"There's nothing to tell," Twitch says, and then walks away.

"You're no fun!" I yell out to him.

I put the lid on the ice cream and put it back in the freezer. I walk over to Axle. "Come on… tell me about Twitch and Milly."

He raises his hands defensively. "I can't. Twitch has already got his panties in a twist from me starting the conversation."

I pout. "You're no fun either."

"Ha! Said no one ever!"

I laugh. "Well… I've got some work to do. I'll be on my laptop in Viper's room."

After I shower and answer emails, I'm on the phone with Maddy, the manager of my nightclub. I breathe a sigh of relief when she confirms the nightclub is running well. No problems at all. "Thanks so much," I tell her. "Remember I'm only a phone call away."

"Everything is perfectly fine. You have nothing to worry about. If there're any problems, I'll manage them. You enjoy your time away."

I make a note to increase her salary. Some employees are worth their weight in gold.

I'm closing my laptop as Viper walks into his room. Perspiration covers his face. His deep breaths make his chest rise and fall. He must have run hard to be breathing like that.

"Thank you for today."

He gives me a half-smile and rakes a hand through his hair. "Your Dad's an asshole."

I peer at the ground and laugh a little. "I'm sorry about that. I should have warned you beforehand. He's full on." I shrug. "In his own twisted way, he wants what's best for me." I flinch… that came out wrong.

"I get it… I do… just print me out that contract so I can prove to the both of you I was never interested in the money."

I pause and clasp my hands in front of me. "What were you interested in then?"

"Everything," he says, smiling. "You own your own business, you're driven, you're confident… and the sass…" He laughs. "I love all the sass. And look at you"—his eyes flicker over me—"you're the most beautiful woman I've ever laid eyes on."

I'm blushing… like bright red, hot cheeks. Giddy excitement rushes through me. I place my hands on my cheeks, attempting to cool them down. "You're biased… you're my husband."

His smile is amplified. "Say that again."

"You're my husband."

His eyes turn dark. His lips slightly part as his tongue creeps out and runs slowly along his bottom lip. I can't take my eyes off him. *All muscly, sweaty.* I peer down at his crotch, where his dick is bulging against his shorts… And *horny.*

He hasn't even kissed me yet and I'm squeezing my thighs against one another to restrict the throb. I stand, then step over to him. He gives me one of his seductive grins. I wrap my arms around him to pull him down to me and kiss him.

His lips are soft and delicious, and our bodies mold together. His hands land on my lower back, then wander to my hips and grip tightly as his kiss deepens when he pushes onto my lips harder. I open my mouth, granting him entry, tilting my head to get better access. When our tongues meet, he groans, and it sends shockwaves to my core.

Our tongues lap and roll, finding the perfect tempo. I thread my fingers through his hair as he presses his groin into my lower stomach, his erection hard. I pull back an inch. "Take me," I whisper against his lips.

He pulls away as I struggle to get air into my lungs. His tongue snakes out and he licks his bottom lip. "You taste so sweet." His voice is a caress against my skin, making me shudder. All that's going through my head right now is *dick… dick… dick…*

With hooded eyes, he says, "Stay married to me." He lowers his hand and grabs his cock. "And then you can have all of me." All of him is huge, and I do… I want all of him… Poisonous thoughts filter through my mind: *I can lie… I can stay married for one extra day… one extra week…* But that's not me. I'm not a liar. I've always been honest, and I don't want to go against my own morals, even though there's a devil on my shoulder saying, "Just this once."

"Fuck you" is on the tip of my tongue, but I swallow it and turn my back to him and walk back over to the bed and sit down. I blow out a series of short breaths to gain control as I try to ease the frustration in my mind and the tension in my body. He studies me and chuckles, wanders over to his wardrobe, grabs some clothes out, and leaves.

I take my phone out and call Piper.

"Hello," she answers. "How's life with the biker?"

I suck in a sharp breath and release my anger. "Viper's cockblocking me. He won't have sex with me until I promise to stay longer or stay married to him or whatever the hell he wants from me. What a joke! At this point, when I leave here, I'll be a virgin again and my hymen will have grown back over."

There's a second of silence before a burst of laughter.

"It's not funny!"

Still laughter… I wait until she stops, mentally slapping myself for allowing Viper to have this much control over my emotions.

"Usually, it's the woman using sex against the man, not the other way around. I can't wait to meet this guy. He sounds hilarious."

"Well, I can assure you he's not," I clip out.

"He's got you in a tailspin, that's for sure… On the other hand, I think you're freaking out that he wants to spend more time with you."

"I'm not freaking out!"

"Yes, you are! You're a control freak, so you never have to get too close. It's why you have two phones and sometimes make up a false name if the guy doesn't know who you are. You've always known you could get any guy you want. And now the one man you really want won't give it up. You got to admit… it's funny… He's your karma."

I let out a long, exaggerated groan, making her chuckle. "And he's so hot. It's not fair. When he kisses me… I just want to rip his clothes off. That deep voice… those full lips… that literal rock-hard muscled body, and his dick is massive. He has a perfect dick to go with his stupid perfect body and his stupid perfect face."

"Oh, stop it," she jokes, "you're making me horny!"

That makes me laugh. The door widens and my jaw drops. Viper struts inside wearing gray sweatpants. GRAY FUCKING SWEATPANTS! That bulge has me rubbing my thighs together *again*! "I've got to go," I say in a tight voice and hang up.

Viper's hair is still wet, drops of water falling on his skin and making its way down his muscles, which are cut to perfection. He even has the V, and his dick… I see every ridge through his pants. My mouth waters. I'm a pooling mess of want. "You," I hiss at him, "suck!" I grab a pillow and throw it at him, which he catches, grinning.

"You're so sexy when you're mad!" The amusement in his voice makes me narrow my eyes at him.

"I hate you!"

His grin intensifies. "No, wifey… You love me!"

I scowl. "You wait! I'll get you back!" A mix of a promise and a threat cut through my tone. I need to get away from him before I do something like attack him. I stand and stomp out of the room. "Evil, evil man," I mutter under my breath.

I wander downstairs, needing to get my mind off him. I

can hear the sweet butts' voices in the kitchen. Trixie is getting pizza out of the oven while Mercedez is putting chicken pieces on a large serving tray. Dolly is in the pantry, while Candy is leaning against the kitchen island, arms crossed over her chest.

"I can't wait until she leaves," Candy whines. "She" I gather is referring to me, so I take a few steps back so I'm out of their view.

There's a long sigh. "Give it a break already," Mercedez says. "At this rate, I'll be glad when she leaves so I don't have to listen to you bitching all day."

"I like her," Trixie adds. "Her lively personality is just what we need here, and she challenges Viper. I think she's exactly what he needs." I clutch my chest.

"You're supposed to be on my side!" Candy's voice is loud.

Trixie replies, "I'm not on anyone's side. I'm just saying what I think."

I peek around the corner to see Dolly walking out with napkins. "Sophie's beautiful; I'm enjoying having her here just to look at."

I can't stop the chuckle that falls from my mouth. All the women's heads turn to me. A blush creeps up Dolly's cheeks.

"Hello," I say in a chirpy voice as I walk toward them.

"Hello," Trixie and Mercedez answer back.

I lean over and reach in front of Candy to grab an apple from the fruit bowl. The apple crunches as I take a bite out of it. She narrows her eyes at me. There's silence until I finish chewing and swallow.

"Viper's a married man now… It's time you moved on."

Her face turns red. She turns on her heels and leaves.

I turn to Dolly. "You're beautiful too, babe."

Her lips curve into a broad smile. I make my way outside and decide I need a girl's day, but with Zara, Ava, and Elena. I call Zara first to ensure they have people to cover for them at the charity tomorrow. Then I organize a spa treatment for all of us. I study my chipped fingernails. I wouldn't mind a massage, a hair wash and blow-dry, and a manicure and pedicure, so I go about making these appointments for us at my family's resort.

ELEVEN
ACHING VAJAYJAY

Sophie

"So, where is this place you want to go?" Rage asks from the driver's side.

"The spa. It's at the Crown Resort, which is by the beach on the main road."

He nods.

"I'm excited," Elena says. She's sitting next to Zara and behind Ava in the back seat.

"How did you get roped into playing chaperone?" I ask Rage.

"The men are extra cautious with their ol' ladies, and I'm the lowest-ranking member."

I reach forward and run my fingers through his lush, soft hair. He pulls away from me.

"Your hair is so soft. Do you want to have a wash and blow-dry too?"

"No." He sounds offended.

"Your loss."

"Leave the poor guy alone," Zara says.

I smile at her. "What? He does have nice hair."

Zara's lips press together as she smothers a smile. "He takes his role seriously."

I quirk a brow. "Watching us get manicures and pedicures? What do the men think, we're going to get waterboarded while a woman washes our hair for us at my family's establishment?"

There are cackles of laughter. The men remind me of my father's overprotectiveness. When we were children, we needed a security guard with us… well, especially me. Even now, in my twenties, he added extra security cameras outside my apartment in New York and a button to press if I'm in distress inside. He even hired a full-time chauffeur to ensure my safety, so I don't need to worry about public transportation.

We pull into the Crown Resort parking lot. The white building has large windows and majestic arches.

"Where do I park?" Rage asks.

"The valet will take your keys, so pull up by the front doors."

He pauses. "Nah. Where else can I park?"

I squint at him. "Why can't you give the valet the keys?"

"No one is getting access to the MC's vehicle."

Fair enough. "Up ahead, past the reception building, you'll see private parking spaces, which are for my family. Park in any one of them."

Rage parks next to Dad's Rolls-Royce and my brother's red Ferrari.

We all get out, meet at the back of the truck, and walk toward the entrance. "Nice cars," Elena points out. "Axle would love them. I can't wait to tell him."

Rage is scanning the perimeter while we walk. The glass doors open wide as we walk through. A familiar security guard is by the door, and a woman is at reception, behind the counter. She smiles up at us. I give her a nod in greeting. "We're booked in for the spa today."

"I'll let them know you're here, Sophie," she says through a smile and picks up the phone.

Ava's and Elena's eyes are wide as they look around the resort. It has a high ceiling with marble floors and a chandelier hanging from the roof. It screams five-star luxury. The room is a mixture of primarily white with touches of gold.

I walk to the elevator and press the button as the others follow me, and when the doors slide open, we all get inside.

"I've seen nothing quite like this here," Ava says, amazed.

"My family doesn't half-ass anything," I reply.

When the elevator doors open, a woman meets us. She's wearing the white spa uniform, her hair is in a bun, her makeup is perfect, and she has the customer service smile. Once we're all out, she says, "My name's Samantha. I'll be one of the therapists assisting you today." She looks between all of us, her smile never wavering. "What service would you like to get done first?"

"Nails and pedicures, please."

She bobs her head. "Follow me."

We walk down a corridor, and she opens a door to a room with four curtained cubicles on one side and lockers on the other. "There's a gown in each cubicle to get changed into and"—she points at the lockers—"these are to put your belongings in. When you're finished, join me outside, and I'll escort you to the salon." She peers at Rage, whose eyes are wide. He looks completely out of his element. "Would you like me to get you a gown?"

"No." His voice is stern, and it makes me laugh. Poor Rage.

After getting changed, Ava is the last one to meet us

outside. She's patting the white fluffy gown at the shoulder. "It's so soft."

We follow the woman past more doors. "What's in these?" Elena asks.

"Massage rooms," I answer her.

"Yeah, about that…" Rage says, so I turn to him. "The men said you're only allowed female massage therapists."

Zara is shaking her head with a small grin.

My lips curve into a devilish smile. "I'm having a man massage me just to annoy Viper. And you make sure you go back and tell him—I'm getting a happy ending." Not that they do that here, and I would never ask for it, anyway.

Rage scratches his forehead. "Do I really have to call him and tell him that?"

"Yes, you do."

He blows out a breath, takes his phone from his pocket, dials, and brings it to his mouth.

The woman leads us to a row of seats that have pedicure bowls filled with water with rose petals floating on top. We all sit. I place my feet into the warm, refreshing water as the woman comes out with glasses of champagne. Ava is the only one to say no.

Rage walks to me and hands me his phone. "It's Viper."

I smile and take the phone from him. "Hello, cockblocker," I say, making the women in the room laugh.

"Oh… Temptress," he says, and I can tell he's smiling. "Remember our deal? We can't be with anyone else."

"Well… I presumed when I got married that getting laid was part of the deal. Since you're not holding up your end… why should I keep mine?"

There's a brief silence. "I will leave now. When I get there, I'll put you over my shoulder and drag you out. Is that what you want? Do you want to be embarrassed like that?" He sounds serious, making me think he might do it. Though good luck with my father's security here.

What to do… what to do… I peer at the women as I contemplate my next move. They are staring at me with curiosity. I haven't even gotten my nails done yet. As fun as it would be, I want to make a day of it with the girls.

"Fine… no happy ending." I act disappointed.

"Atta girl. And wifey?"

"Hmm…"

"No male is to touch that pretty skin of yours."

I snort. "If that's the case, you need to stop depriving your wife of sex."

"Sophie," he warns. Ohhhhh, he used my first name. He must be serious.

"Yes, hubby… I promise."

"Have a good day!"

"Thank you. We will."

I hold my hand out to pass the phone back to Rage, who then talks to Viper, who's probably making sure Rage doesn't leave my side.

I glance around to see the women holding back grins.

"What? It's not fair! He still won't have sex with me," I deadpan.

"It's so weird!" says Elena.

"He thinks his big dick and teasing will make me cave. I'm trying to be strong, but it's a struggle… you know."

Everyone laughs again.

"I'm glad my aching vajayjay is amusing to all of you but mark my words: I will get him back!" I need to figure out what will be payback to him but entertaining for me. I think it's only right I get something out of it too.

"Your wedding is in a few months'; do you need me to help in any way?" says Ava to Zara.

My eyes brighten, and I rub my hands together. "Your Wedding! That's so exciting. I can't wait."

"Mom and I have organized most of it, but if I think of anything, I'll let you know. We will need help on the day of the wedding," Zara replies.

"Make sure you let me know too. I'll be happy to help." My smile falls. I may be back in New York by the time she needs help. That sucks! I guess I can still help on the day of the wedding.

Our day goes by way too quickly, but when we're finished, I'm feeling like a new person. When we walk out of the elevator in the lobby, the security guard steps toward me, places a hand on my elbow, and ushers me away. "Your father would like to see you."

Rage appears at my side and pulls me behind him. The security guard lets go. Rage stands at full height, his body rigid. "Don't touch her."

The security guard is as tall as Rage but more solid. I move in front of them, putting my hand on Rage's chest. "It's okay, my dad wants to see me."

His shoulders fall ever so slightly. Then he looks at me. "Would you like me to come?"

I give him a small smile. "I won't be long."

"But Viper said I can't leave you."

"This behemoth here," I say, nodding at the security guard, "will walk me to my father."

Rage's facial expression is tight.

"Her family owns this resort; she'll be safe," Zara says confidently. Rage nods, even though his body is stiff.

I turn and walk back into the elevator with the security guard, who presses the button. When the elevator doors open, we walk side by side until we reach my father's office. He's in his chair, looking out the window at the beach.

The security guard knocks on the door, and I walk inside.

My father stands to greet me. I kiss his cheek and step away. "Hi, Dad. Is there something you need from me?"

"It's good to see you again." He doesn't give me time to reply. "I haven't received the signed contract, though I'm not surprised he hasn't signed it. He's in it for the money, Sophie!"

Big breath in… and out, though it does nothing to ease the tightness in my chest. "You'll receive it soon."

The shake of his head and the clear disappointment in his eyes pain me. "I don't trust him, and frankly, I'm concerned about your recent decisions and lack of urgency on the matter."

My upper body tenses, then drops. "I'll get the contract to you shortly. I don't want to keep the women waiting." I love my father, but he tests me. "I'd better get going. Bye, Dad."

"I'll talk to you soon," he says as I'm leaving the room.

We walk back inside the clubhouse to raised voices. "You played me!" a woman yells.

"I never said we were together!" I know that voice. It's Viper.

I walk down the hallway to see Candy and Viper glaring at each other. Axle, Demon, and Twitch have drinks in their hands, looking thoroughly amused watching the commotion, while Bomber, Reaper, and Cash are playing pool. The men smile when we walk in. Ava steps into Reaper's arms, Elena plops onto Axle's lap, and Zara gives Bomber a brief kiss on the lips. Rage walks straight to the bar. Poor guy probably needs a strong drink.

Candy glances our way, and as soon as her eyes meet mine, she gives me a death stare. "Oh, great…" she throws her hands up. "Your so-called wife is back."

"Calm your tits!" I lift my hand, showing the ring on my finger. "And I'm not a *so-called* wife. I *am* his wife."

Candy shifts back to Viper and slaps his chest. "I was supposed to be your endgame!"

My heart pounds. I rush over, stand in front of him, and push her back. "You don't touch him!" *He's mine.* Protectiveness swirls inside of me.

Viper's arms are around me, holding me back when all I want to do is hit the bitch for laying hands on him.

Mercedez is by Candy's side. "Come for a walk with me to calm down."

"Candy!" Reaper's voice carries over. Everyone looks at him. "This is your last chance. I see you acting like that again toward anyone living under our roof and I won't hesitate to throw your ass out and ban you for life."

She pales. Mercedez directs Candy outside. Viper grabs my hips and turns me around to face him. He has one of his grins on his face, but adrenaline is still firing through my veins.

"You let her touch you like that?" I say through deep breaths. He chuckles, and it irks me.

"Everything's okay. I think she needed to get her anger out and tell me what she wanted to say."

I shake my head. "She touches you like that again… I'll slap her back. She needs to be brought down a level."

He leans down, his mouth going to my ear, where I feel his warm breath. "Seeing you all feisty has made me hard…"

My breath catches. He places his hand in mine and pulls me away up the stairs. My heart beats faster with every step. *Finally!*

"Do you have something serious going on with Candy?" We stride to his room. He pulls me inside and pushes me on the bed. I fall back, jumping slightly against the mattress.

As he takes my shorts off, he says, "Look, we never said we were in a relationship. Hell, she knew I screwed other women. But yeah, we had sex a lot too. It was easy and convenient."

Jealousy cuts me, but Viper continues, "Sex brought me pleasure… made me feel loved even, during it. I was in foster care growing up… so I guess I was always searching for that feeling, and maybe I should have stopped having sex with her when I knew she was into me."

The vulnerability in his voice when talking about growing up in foster care makes my chest ache.

He rips my thong, letting the thin fabric flutter to the floor. "Now you know… so no more talking about Candy."

The need to have him in me is getting the better of me. He pulls my legs, making me squeal as my ass shifts to the edge of the bed.

He opens my legs wide, his tongue snaking out as he licks his lips. His eyes run appreciatively down my body and settle at the juncture of my thighs. "Perfect and pink." His voice is gravelly, and his eyes hold a promise of what's to come. "And all mine."

A turmoil of emotions battle within me—frustration, desire, and anger. He kneels in front of me and everything revs, clenches, and grows slick with need. His tongue slips in. The invasion makes me gasp. He licks a delicious stroke up my middle. One of his hands pins my thigh open; his mouth is firm. Pleasure ricochets through me, and nothing else matters but his mouth on me.

"Oh… Viper," I moan as my grip tightens on his hair.

His talented mouth sucks and dances on my clit, then explores every inch of me with leisurely licks before delving in deep. There's a surge of pressure going from my tummy to my core.

"That's it!" I cry, pushing my hips forward onto his mouth, desperate for release.

My breaths are harsh and fast as I tremble with the

onslaught of pleasure. The building pressure makes me reach the peak. My world shatters as my violent climax blasts through me, making my body bow and releasing my frustration.

Without giving me time to come down from the high, he slams one finger into me, stretching me. "Viper," I say through pants, "I haven't recovered yet." But my muscles clench around his finger in greedy delight.

He pulls out only to push in two fingers, deeper, expertly curling and stroking, eliciting pleasure. The rhythm is relentless. Torturous sparks of bliss shoot through me. I feel the buildup of another orgasm.

When he works my sensitive clit with his thumb, my body jerks, but then I'm squirming and bucking.

"Come again for me," his gravelly voice demands.

"Yes!" I yell because I'm nearly there.

With a firm press of his thumb and a deep thrust, he says, "Come."

I burst apart, thrashing my head from side to side as another climax rips through me, making me scream out and see an explosion of stars. I ripple around him, milking him with every wave of release. My heart hammers and I'm boneless, my body lax against the bed. As I drift down from the high, I let out a long, satisfied sigh.

"You're good," I mumble through heavy breaths. *Thank the Lord.*

He stands and flashes a wide smile. "Yeah, I am."

He puts the two fingers that were inside of me in his mouth. His eyes burn as he sucks off the remaining traces of my orgasm. It's the hottest thing I've ever seen. As I look at his gorgeous face, I realize he has the potential to break my heart, and for once… I'm not feeling the need to run. My heart beats faster at that, but I blame the post-orgasmic feeling for making me think that.

TWELVE
GOOD DICK... CHECK

Sophie

EVEN THOUGH I WAS DELICIOUSLY EATEN OUT YESTERDAY, IT hasn't satisfied my hunger for him. He must be getting himself off somewhere, otherwise he would be walking around with a boner twenty-four-seven. After our morning run, I speak to the manager at my club, who jokingly tells me, yet again, everything is fine.

I sit in Viper's room, blankly staring at my laptop screen. I need to figure out what will make him cave. What would it take to make him throw his manipulative ways to the wind and finally have sex with me? Well… he didn't want the massage therapist's hands on me. Maybe jealousy is my way out.

My phone rings. I pick it up from the bed, glance at the screen, and bring it to my ear. "Hello, Lawson."

"Hey… how's the wilderness?"

"I haven't come across any wild animals yet, though they keep a dog here that's the size of a mountain lion."

He laughs. "How's Viper?"

"A literal pain in my vagina."

"Eww, Sophie... I never want to hear that word coming out of your mouth again."

I grin. "What have you been up to?"

"I just got back last night from the international whiskey competition. My whiskey placed first in the Whiskey of the Year category."

"Congratulations!" I beam. I'm so proud of him. Even though the whiskey distillery has been in our family for generations, it wasn't until Lawson started to manage it and perfect the recipe and the process that it started to get the recognition it deserves.

"I was planning a party tonight to celebrate."

"I'll be there," I'm quick to reply. "Where are you thinking of having it?"

"Here at the resort, in the event room, seven p.m."

"Do you need me to organize anything for you?" I offer.

"No, I'll get the event planner to organize it. You can invite Viper, Bomber, and Zara if you want."

"Sure... Can you book my normal room at the resort so that me, Zara, and the guys can drink and go back to the room afterward?"

"I can do that. See you tonight, sis."

I call Zara, knowing she'll be at the charity.

"Hello," she answers.

"Are you and Bomber free tonight? My brother is celebrating his win at the international whiskey competition. He came first in one of the categories."

She gasps. "That's amazing. Count us in."

"I've organized a room each for us to stay in, in case the men want to drink."

"Sounds great. I'm excited!"

My smile beams. "Me too!"

"What time?"

"At seven," I answer.

"Would you like for us to travel together?" Zara asks.

"Yes, that would be easier."

After getting off the phone, I hear loud cracks coming from outside. The men must be having target practice or something.

When I go downstairs, Cash is placing bottles of beer in the bar fridge and spirits up on the cabinets. I wander over to him, and because I'm in a mood, I decide to annoy him.

"Hello, Mr. Tall, Dark, and Handsome. Can I have a whiskey and cola?"

He turns to me with a smile. "Sure." He really is handsome, with his dark features, trimmed beard, and easygoing smile.

He picks up another whiskey brand. "No, no. Crown Village whiskey. My brother just got awarded first place in the international whiskey awards for it."

His brows lift, and he grasps the Crown Village whiskey instead. "That's awesome." After pouring a shot, the cola is next. "I didn't know you're a big drinker," he says with a tinge of amusement.

I laugh. "I try to eat healthy and exercise, but I also like my drinking… it's all about balance." Well… that's what I tell myself.

He places my drink in front of me. My eyes wander around his chest. His white fitted shirt fits snugly, with his leather cut over the top.

"Straw?"

He cocks his head. "We don't have any."

"Well… you better put that on the grocery list. Have you ordered my ol' lady's cut yet?" I ask teasingly.

He subtly shakes his head, with the touch of a smile on his face. "Viper hasn't requested it."

I bring the drink to my lips and take a sip, enjoying the smooth rich flavor. "But I have!"

He slowly raises his hands. "Only patched members can request them."

I quirk my brow.

"Don't shoot the messenger!" he says playfully.

That makes me smile. "Where are the women?"

"Ava's at college. Elena and Axle went out for the day, and Zara is at the charity."

"Do you have a woman?"

His head inches back, and there's a stiffness in his body I haven't seen before.

"What? Am I not allowed to ask personal questions?"

"No… I don't have one." His voice is void of emotion.

His response makes me curious. I'm surprised someone hasn't snatched him up. "Did you ever meet *the one*?"

There's a tightness in his jaw. *Oops, I've hit a nerve.* But I have so many questions, I can't stop myself. "I'll take that as a yes. Where is she?" Knowing he's been in the military… he would be in his twenties. "Let me guess, high school sweetheart?"

With a set jaw, he wipes down the counter. "Something like that."

Viper struts toward us with the cocky grin that I love. His mix of confidence and sex appeal makes me squirm in my seat. *Far out—I need to get laid.* He takes a seat next to me. His eyes are bouncing between me and Cash, then linger on Cash a little longer.

Viper is quite observant because he frowns then looks at me. "What did you say to him?" he asks accusingly.

Cash lets out an uncomfortable chuckle. "It's all good."

"Wifey…" Viper warns.

"What?" I ask super sweetly.

"You need to keep out of other people's business. We don't like to talk about our feelings."

"I can't help it. I'm nosey. By the way, we've got a party to attend tonight."

He slowly raises a brow. "Really? Whose party?"

"My brother Lawson. He won an international award for his whiskey, so he's celebrating."

His eyes widen. "Good on him."

"Lawson told me to ask Bomber and Zara, so I've already spoken to Zara about it and organized us a room each to sleep in, so we can all drink."

"Where's it at?"

"The resort," I answer.

He pauses, then his face falls. "So that means your dad is going to be there."

I frown. "It's important for Lawson, so just ignore Dad."

His face softens. "Yeah, I know. I'll deal with your dad." Viper's surprisingly handling my family, my lifestyle, and my extroverted personality well.

THE DAY GOES BY QUICKLY. AT SIX-THIRTY P.M., I'M TOUCHING UP my makeup. I'm going with a summer glow, natural makeup, with my blonde hair in waves and a white embroidered wrap dress with white Louboutin shoes. To add the final touches, I'm wearing a white lace lingerie set with garters and stockings. If he doesn't have sex with me tonight, he either is desperate to stay married or he might be getting his needs met elsewhere. The thought burns.

There's a light knock on the door. "Sophie, are you ready yet?" Zara's soft voice filters through. I sling my bag over my shoulder, step toward the door, and open it wide. "Woah," she says. "You look beautiful. Viper won't be able to keep his hands off of you."

I smile back. "That's the plan." She chuckles.

Zara is naturally stunning; her long midnight hair is straight. She's wearing a fitted black dress with a princess neckline with a deep V. The dress falls to just below her knees.

I link my arm with hers, and we walk together through the hallway and down the stairs. We're met with whistling and cheering, mainly from the women but also from a few of the men. As I let go of Zara, I notice the pink in her cheeks.

Bomber strides to her and wraps his hands around her as he kisses her on the lips. I search for Viper. He's at the bar. He tosses back a shot before he comes over wearing one of his charming grins. I don't miss the heat in his eyes as they greedily feast on my body. His lust-filled gaze pins me in place. It's enough for me to overheat with desire.

He stands and moves behind me, snaking his arms over my hips and bringing me flush against him. His fingers dig in… his head lowers to my ear… his breath flutters on my ear and neck. "How am I going to last the evening with you looking like this?" His voice is low and seductive.

Triumph flares inside me as I slowly turn in his grip. I loop my arms around his neck and whisper, "You're not supposed to."

"Are you two going to make it to the resort?"

I'd know that smartass voice anywhere. I giggle as I shift, bringing my arms down and stepping out of Viper's hold to peek at Axle. "We will because your friend"—I stare Viper down before finishing—"won't have sex with his wife."

Axle's mouth is on the floor. Cash and Rage's eyes flash wide. *Yeah, that's right…* At least I'm not the only one surprised by Viper's sudden abstinence.

Viper shakes his head, avoiding eye contact with everyone

else but looking from me to Zara to Bomber. "Who's driving?"

"I am," Bomber replies.

I sway my hips all the way to the truck. Viper opens the door for me. The gentlemanly act makes me smile. He holds his hand out, and I grasp it as he helps me get up and into the back seat. When the truck moves down the driveway, I sense Viper's intense stare, and when I turn to him, his focus is on my dress.

He reaches out to touch the edge of the fabric near my knees. Pinching the material between his fingers, he slowly brings it up my thigh, grazing my leg, making me shiver. His fingers ever so gently move my dress up and make their way to the top of my thigh. His eyebrows draw in as he pulls my dress up higher. He groans when he reaches the point where my stockings are linked to lacy suspenders, then his mouth clamps shut and his jaw clenches.

"What's wrong?" I ask, feigning innocence.

He pulls on the stockings and they spring back into place. His hand slides higher, making my breath quicken. His heated eyes penetrate mine. "You're going to be the death of me."

I can't wait for him to see the crotchless underwear I'm wearing. His hand firmly grasps my thigh, and his body stays rigid the rest of the way.

When we park at the resort, Viper goes around, opens the door and helps me down. He, Bomber, and Zara follow me to the event room, where it's a cocktail-style event with guests standing with drinks in hand. The waitresses and waiters, dressed up in white and black, are going around with trays of food.

I sense eyes on us, and when I quickly survey the area, I notice a nearby group giving Viper and Bomber a cautious glance. Everyone else is dressed up, whereas they're wearing jeans and shirts with their cuts over the top. The men stand out, but I can't imagine Viper wearing anything else.

I spot Lawson shaking hands and laughing with friends. I step to the side and see Harrison talking to people, but when Harrison's eyes land on me he smiles and waves me over, so I go to him.

"Hey, sis." I step into his outstretched arms and give him a brief hug.

"How have you been?" I ask.

"Good."

Viper steps up beside me. He's smiling at Harrison. "Hey," he says, and they shake hands.

"How's my sister treating you?" Harrison asks with a twinkle in his eye.

Viper glances at me before answering. "Wifey has been great, I couldn't imagine my life without her." The sincerity in his voice makes my breath catch.

"Aww…" Zara says from next to me.

"Congratulations. I'm glad you two"—Harrison's eyes stay on me a little longer—"are making a go of it."

I'm in a daze while Harrison greets Zara and Bomber. My chest is tight at Viper's declaration. The storm of mixed emotions scares me.

Alec makes his way to us, with his domineering presence and buzzkill persona. I smile at him. "Sophie," he says, giving me a tight nod but shakes hands with the men. I have no idea what Piper sees in him. It must solely be based on looks because if she really knew him, she wouldn't like my grumpy brother.

"You're still here," Alec says to me. "I thought you'd be divorced and gone by now."

"Why wouldn't I still be here?" I sound irritated.

He lifts a brow and purses his lips. "You hate Crown

Village, and going from New York to a rural area, I didn't think you'd cope."

It's not that I hate this place. When I finished school, I had to move away. I needed my own life, my own identity away from my family. Now, I'm enjoying being back.

Viper links his hand in mine, which makes me glance at him, while he speaks to Alec. "She's doing well. Can multi-task managing her business while spending time and building friendships with the women and men in the club-house. She's extraordinary, and I'm one lucky bastard to have her."

Our group is suddenly quiet. The heaviness from Alec's presence floats away. Viper sees me for who I am. I stand taller.

Harrison laughs. "I can see why you're such a hit with the ladies."

"I'm a married man now." Viper used to be a player, but his eyes have never wandered to anyone else.

I have a feeling that there're people behind us. "Hello…" Harrison says to a group of four men—all tall, handsome, and muscular. Viper's hand tightens on mine.

"I'm glad you guys made it." Harrison turns to me. "These are some of my fellow firefighters."

I go to give them a hug, but my hand is firmly in Viper's, and he isn't letting go. I give the firefighters a bright smile instead. Harrison peers down at our hands and chuckles under his breath.

"I'm going to chat with Lawson," I tell the group, then Viper and I move through the crowd toward Lawson.

"Better watch who you bat those eyelashes at."

I pause and peer up at Viper. There's a lightness to his voice, a tilt of a lip, but the intensity of his gaze says other-wise. My inner bitch rears her head. I place my other hand on his chest and look him dead in the eyes while lowering my voice. "If you don't have sex with me… someone else will."

Viper raises a brow. His grin spreads. "I'd like to see them try."

What an arrogant husband I have. I didn't think this through. Just the thought of sex makes me wet. I raise a brow right back at him. "You want to make a bet on that?"

His smile dims and his eyes tighten. I hold back a smirk.

"Let's get one thing straight." His voice is raspy but firm. "I don't share." Those words cut straight to my core. I don't know why I'm getting aroused by being each other's only one. *I'm unraveling.*

I give him my best seductive smile while placing his hand on my thigh, loving the way his hand feels on my bare skin. I lean up on my toes to whisper in his ear. "I'm wearing crotch-less underwear," I tease, quietly, so only he can hear.

Lawson sees us and walks over. I hug him. "Congratulations," I say in an upbeat voice. "I'm so proud of you."

He smiles. "I couldn't believe it when they called out my name." He chuckles. "I think I'm still in shock."

He glances at Viper, who's turned to stone. "Is he okay?" he asks me, and it makes me giggle.

"I don't think he's feeling too well," I mumble in amusement.

"He looks pale," Lawson remarks, and I laugh again, which makes my brother give me an odd expression. He's probably thinking I'm laughing because Viper is sick when he's not… but I can't explain that.

I place a hand on Viper's arm, which breaks him out of his daze. "Do you want me to take you somewhere so you can lie down?" I try to keep the mischief out of my voice but fail miserably.

"Lawson," someone calls out to my brother.

"I'll catch you guys later," he says before he leaves us.

When I glance back at Viper, I still. The sexual tension between us makes my heart race, and I'm suffocating in his presence.

"Fuck it!" Viper says under his breath, and the surrender in his eyes makes my body ache for him. He grasps my arm tightly, and we cross the room in quick strides. Excitement is injected into my veins.

There's a door off to the side, by the entrance to the event room, and he pulls me inside, making me gasp. The small room is lined with jackets and coats. I'd never paid much attention to this small room until now.

My back is flush against the door. His arm comes out beside me, and I hear the door lock.

His predatory gaze lights me on fire, and I'm burning alive. "Fuck you for making me cave," he says heatedly. He's panting heavily. I can't respond because his lips are on mine, hot and all-consuming, then he thrusts his tongue in. Desperate for anything he has to give, I kiss him back with the same feverishness. We kiss like we're strung out and we're each other's drug.

A growl rips from his chest. He peels his jeans down, freeing himself. When he picks me up, I wrap my legs around his hips and throw my arms around his neck, over his cut, though our mouths never leave each other. Our tongues dance, and we take from each other over and over. He grabs my ass and lines us up and pushes inside of me, sinking in to the hilt. We both groan.

I stretch exquisitely to accommodate his wide girth. I'm assaulted with both pleasure and pain.

"So wet…" he says huskily against my lips. "So tight… Mine!"

My head falls back against the door. There's six feet of solid muscle against me, thrusting deeply. We have our clothes on—only our intimate parts are connected—but it feels too intimate, as we're eye to eye. With every thrust, he's claiming me.

His head inches back. "You drive me crazy," he says breathlessly. "I'm going to come so hard inside you." His voice is threaded with lust and a hint of agony.

His declaration sends a burst of warmth through me. As he pumps his hips, sweat mists my skin. I can sense the scorching heat emanating from him through his clothes.

Wild for him, I moan as he consumes me over and over with short thrusts and pounds my body into submission. His brown eyes are wild. My blood is roaring in my ears, with every punishing stroke drawing me closer to the edge.

Everything tightens. My orgasm explodes through me as his rhythm increases in pace. A roar tears from his chest, and he pulses inside of me. His movements slow, and we are both breathing heavily, coming down from our high, the scent of sex heavy in the air.

His eyes roam my face, and the side of his lip tilts up. "You're so fucking sexy like this, I want to stay buried inside of you."

I crack a smile. My chest is rising and falling. "About time… That's what I needed."

He slowly pulls out, gently lowering me to my feet. On shaky legs, I fan myself. "Woah!" His seed drips out of me. "Quick, I need something to wipe myself with."

He steps to me and places a firm, fierce kiss on my lips. As he pulls away, I sigh, wanting round two.

"I want you walking around with my cum inside of you so that everyone knows who you belong to."

My mouth gapes, my heart flutters, and my pussy clenches. *This man…* He moves away from me and I step to the side, biting my lip as I feel him run down my leg.

He opens the door and quirks a brow. "You ready?"

I swallow hard and nod. "Yes."

He places his hand in mine and tugs me over to him. Before he steps outside the door, he looks me over. "You look thoroughly fucked," he says proudly.

After hours of drinking and dancing, I'm feeling beyond tipsy. I wash my hands after going to the bathroom and look at myself in the mirror. I smile. I love spending time with my family and the MC.

As I'm walking out, I see my father has made an appearance. He's talking to Bomber and Viper. Their bodies are stiff while Dad's talking to them. I rush over when Dad points a finger at Viper.

When Viper's eyes meet mine, he forces a smile. My eyes dart between the three of them. "What's going on?"

"Nothing," Dad answers, though Bomber's jaw is ticking.

Viper casually puts his arm around my shoulders. "Are you ready to go soon?"

Noticing the awkward tension, I reply, "Sure…"

"Where's Zara?" I ask Bomber.

He tips his head to the right where she's talking to Lawson. I look between Viper and Bomber. "Are we staying the night here?"

"No. I'm good to drive," Bomber answers, an edge to his voice.

"You've been drinking," Dad says disapprovingly. "The chauffeur can take you."

Bomber's glare is hostile. Something has just gone down, and I want to know what it was. I have a feeling Dad started it. "I've had one beer," Bomber answers.

Dad looks at me. "You should stay with your family."

Viper curses under his breath.

"Zara," Bomber calls out. "We're going."

My eyes peer between them warily. "What's happened?"

Dad fiddles with his tie. "It was business."

I peek under my lashes at Viper. "Let's get going, wifey."

I shuffle my weight between my feet. "I'm going back to the clubhouse. Dad, I'll come and see you again soon."

I hastily say bye, not wanting to cause a scene. I find my brothers and say goodbye before I walk to the parking lot, head bowed. I just wanted a good night with everyone.

THIRTEEN
QUITE THE DILEMMA

Viper

THE RIDE HOME WAS SILENT, BUT I COULD SENSE THE TENSION IN the air. Neither me nor Bomber was going to say anything to the women, but they could sense that something wasn't right. We ended up having an early night, but there was distance between me and Sophie because I wouldn't tell her what's wrong.

After we wake up, Sophie's still drilling me about it. "There's nothing you need to worry about," I say reassuringly. I follow it up with one of my charming smiles. She's smart. She picked up on the vibes between us and her father. "I'm going to church. I'll be back soon."

She purses those sexy, full lips. She's frustrated with me and gives me a look that implies we will talk about this later. She's been here for nearly a week. It's gone so fast. I frown at the thought that I have only three more weeks with her.

I go downstairs, allowing her to work on her laptop. Bomber is waiting for me. "Are you ready?" I ask him. My heart pumps harder. *This is my fault.* I'm the one causing issues with the club because I can't let Sophie go.

"Yes, we have to keep everyone up to date with what's happening," he answers.

"Reaper," I call out when I see him talking to Ava in the dining area. He looks up at me. "Can we talk at church? It's important."

He studies me, then gives me a sharp chin lift. "I'll round them up," he replies.

Bomber and I go toward the room church is held in. He opens the heavy wooden door, and we walk in and sit in our usual spots on either side of Reaper's chair.

The men filter in, taking their seats around the table. I feel their curious stares on us until Reaper takes a seat at the head of the table.

"Bomber and Viper, you have the floor."

"Me and Bomber were at Sophie's brother's celebration party, and Garrett was there. He's still pissed off with me for being married to his daughter." There are chuckles around the table.

"He's run out of patience and wants me out of her life. So far, he's warned me there could be blowback on the club if Sophie stays married to me. He offered me ten grand to get a divorce at the party, but I turned him down. I don't give a shit about the cash." I run my hand down the back of my neck and let out a heavy breath. "I want to stay married to Sophie."

I let out an uncomfortable chuckle. "As you can imagine, it didn't go down well. He looked shocked when I didn't accept it. He's not someone who people say no to often. The conversation got heated because I wasn't budging. So, it went from negotiation to threats." I take a moment as nausea twists my stomach.

"Garrett's made it clear that if me and Sophie don't separate, the police will be at every fight we host, and he'll ensure our shipment won't make it out of town."

Deep voices murmur around the table as the tension heightens. Everyone knows if Garrett gets the police to stop our shipment because we aren't licensed, we could do time. Garrett could tell the police to raid our property at any time, and again, we could end up in jail for growing heaps of weed.

"You're married now, which makes Sophie a part of the MC family. Did you give any thought to how you're going to proceed?" Reaper asks.

"Sophie has three weeks to decide if she wants to stay married to me, so she might decide for us. If she chooses to leave, everything can go back to the way it was, but then I lose her. Either way, I'm screwed."

I glance around the table once more, looking every man in the eye. "Know that I'd never put the club in this position for just anyone. I've fallen for her, and she's the first woman I've wanted to stay with."

Axle puts his hand on my shoulder. "We know."

"Just get rid of her," Demon says in an emotionless voice. I get it—I would think the same thing if it were anybody else.

"*I can't…*" I say softly. "But I'll come up with a plan to deal with Garrett."

An evil smirk creeps onto Demon's face.

"What?" I ask him curiously.

"I'll thrive in jail, but I'm not sure how you'll do."

I puff out a breath of air. "I'd handle jail just fine." Not that it will get that far… well, I hope not, anyway.

"With that face of yours"—Demon's lips curve higher—"you'll be an inmate's bitch within a day!"

I shake my head at him. "Fuck off!"

"Ohhh… Demon's got jokes," Axle mocks.

"This is a serious threat," Bomber says. "My uncle is not a patient man."

"Just give me some time. I'll think of something," I say confidently, though doubt sits heavy on my chest.

After church, I do a sweep of the house but don't see Sophie, so I briskly go upstairs. When I open the door to my room, she's still on her laptop.

She glances at me. "Are you going to tell me yet?"

I let out a sigh and sit down beside her. I wonder whether I should tell her. Maybe she'll be able to convince her father to change his mind.

"Your father threatened us that if I don't end it with you, he'll shut down the fights we run and stop our pot making it out of town." She sucks in a breath, and I continue. "So, if he wants, we could all end up in jail or, at the very least, lose our buyer. We obviously need to earn an income somewhere, and they tide us over."

"I'll talk to him," she says. "Why the fights and pot though?"

I chuckle. "We're bikers. You won't see us working in suits in nine-to-five jobs. We aren't interested in going back to college or going into the civilian workforce. We didn't want to do what other MCs are doing, like get involved in running guns or moving hard drugs. We also didn't want to be involved in other activities like murder, loan sharking, prostitution, or moving stolen goods."

Her mouth presses into a firm line.

"It is what it is, and your family grants us the ability to run the fights and move the pot out of this town, but they can also stop us, make us go broke, or put us in jail if they want to."

She sighs. "I'll print that contract my dad sent, and if we sign it, it may change his mind so that he stops blackmailing the MC." She does not sound convincing. I'm sure the contract is to prove to Sophie I only wanted her money, but his end goal is for us to separate.

I wrinkle my nose. "Why does he care so much?" I ask, observing her. She's an adult. It blows my mind he's interfering so much.

"It's everything. He's protective of me and thinks being with you is dangerous. He doesn't trust you." She shuts her laptop and sits up straighter. "I don't want to talk about it anymore. What about you? Tell me more about your past."

Maybe, if I gave her insight into my world, we could grow closer. "What do you want to know about me?"

A glint of interest glows in her eyes. A part of me is thrilled she wants to get to know me, but there's nothing special about my past, before the MC.

"I know nothing about you, so anything." She answers.

I clear my throat. "Well… Child Protective Services took me from my family when I was young. My parents couldn't raise me. They were into drugs and had mental health issues, so I bounced from one foster home to the next until I was old enough to enlist in the military.

"The military was where I fit in and made friends with Bomber and Reaper. After serving for many years, we decided to make a life for ourselves outside the military. We knew other veterans were struggling, so we created an MC. It provided us with a place to call home."

She looks away before asking, "Where'd you get the name Viper from?"

My lip tilts in a roguish grin. "As you know, I'm cunning."

A small smile breaks out at the edges of her mouth. "And manipulative," she announces. "Did you plan for us to get married, or was that a fluke?"

I lean back. "From the first time I saw you, I started to plan how to make you mine."

She moves forward and playfully whacks me.

"You can't tell me you've hated being here at the MC with me—and Zara and Bomber. I've noticed you getting along with other club members and their ol' ladies. I saw you grinning when you were with your brothers, so you must be happy about spending time with them in Crown Village."

Something flickers across her face. "Have you been in any long-term relationships?" she asks.

"I was never interested in anything more than sex. I never found anyone I was willing to commit to. Why aren't *you* married?" I ask her.

"I was busy. Modeling had me traveling a lot. Then I wanted to concentrate on my business. Marriage was never a priority. I'd rather go out with friends and hook up with a random."

"Sounds like you've got commitment issues," I say, amused.

She whacks me again, making me laugh. "Sounds like you do too."

I shrug. "I guess so. The flirting and the sex gave me a temporary high…"

She lets out a long sigh. "I understand. I only wanted the sex… nothing else." She shivers. "I don't like being put in a position where I feel vulnerable."

"Vulnerable how?" I ask cautiously.

She looks away, but I saw the sadness in her eyes.

"You can tell me," I say encouraging her to open up.

"Being hurt again… like my parents hurt me. One rejected me, and the other is controlling and difficult to have a relationship with." She looks back at me and attempts to smile. "Anyway… Look at us talking like an old married couple."

"Well… we are married, wifey."

"That we are… that we are… Talking about that, do you have any photos from the night we got married?"

I pull my phone out of my pocket, ecstatic she's showing interest, and open the photo album and pass it to her. She grasps it, then smiles as she swipes left. "Aww…" she coos and puts her hand out to show me the photo. It's a selfie of us smiling. Even though she looks drunk, with glassy eyes, she still looks hot as fuck.

She brings the phone back to her face. Then her eyes widen and her nose crinkles in disgust.

"What photo are you up to?" I ask curiously.

"Us at the altar at some cheap chapel."

"I didn't give a shit where we got married…" *Just that we did.* "That place was the closest to where we were."

"That's a nice photo of me and the girls." She peeks up at me. "I've been meaning to ask you, is Ava pregnant? She didn't drink that night, and every time I've made drinks, she's asked for mocktails."

"They haven't formally announced it, but I think she is. It's only a matter of time before everyone catches on, if they haven't already."

She swipes again and peers down at her hand, then narrows her eyes at me. "I can't believe I got a tattoo."

Even if we break up, she'll always have that on her skin to remind her of me.

"What are you smiling at?" she asks, suspicion lining her voice.

"Nothin'."

She pauses, searching my eyes before going back to the phone. "Good Lord, I look drunk. You got me when I was down. These photos remind me of *The Hangover*, but the tame version where at the end of the movie, they're going through all the photos of that crazy night."

After our morning run, I catch Ava's SUV coming up the driveway. "I'll meet you two inside," I say to Sophie and

Rage. I wait off to the side and watch as the vehicle parks. Reaper gets out, gives me a nod, then goes to Ava's side, opens the door for her, and holds out his hand so she can get down and onto the ground safely.

"When are you going to tell everyone Ava's pregnant?"

Both their heads whip up at me. Ava goes pink in the cheeks, and Reaper shakes his head at me. "You miss nothing!"

"It's obvious to anyone paying attention."

Reaper and Ava walk toward me. "I was worried about telling anyone… I didn't want to jinx it," Ava says.

I put my arms around her. "Congratulations."

She sniffles. "Thank you." She starts blinking rapidly. "These damn hormones!"

I shake hands with Reaper. "Congrats, pres." He smiles a genuine smile. I can see how proud he is.

"Oh! That reminds me." Ava turns back and pulls something small out of her bag. She peels off the back, goes to the driver's side, and sticks it to the driver's side window.

"What sticker did you just put on your car?" I ask.

She nods her head at the sticker, as if happy with it. "It says, 'Don't park too close… I'm chunky!'"

"Beautiful, I love your curves," Reaper says.

"Well… I'm getting *curvier* by the day."

He gives her an adoring smile. "Well… I suppose it's time to tell the rest of the MC now and show them bub's scans."

We go inside and Reaper gets everyone together in the dining room. We all stand around, with Reaper and Ava at the front. Reaper clears his throat. "Me and Ava have some news." They pause and gaze at each other before he speaks. "Ava's pregnant."

Squeals, gasps, and cheers echo around the room. The women all rush to Ava. By Zara's and Elena's lack of surprise,

I gather they already knew. Reaper steps over to the men, where there's a round of congratulations and handshakes.

"Give me a look at the baby's first selfie," Axle says loudly. Ava hands him some images.

"Boy or girl?" I ask, raising my voice over everyone talking.

"We want it to be a surprise," Ava responds.

I laugh. "I bet you it's a girl!" Reaper's eyes narrow, then he briefly closes them and takes a deep breath, making me laugh again. A daughter would be hard enough to bring into this world, let alone the daughter of a military veteran and the president of an MC. If it's a girl, I already pity her.

Afterward, Sophie sashays over to me and stands beside me. Her eyes are on Reaper and Ava. "Do you want kids?" she asks.

I blow out a breath that puffs out my cheeks. I was not expecting her to ask that. "Not really..." I study her face, knowing it could be a deal breaker for some women.

"Me neither," she replies, and my chest loosens.

She glances at me. "Any reason why?"

"It's never interested me, and I've never felt a need to have them. I'm happy to play uncle." I tilt my head toward Ava.

Sophie smiles. "I feel the same way. I don't have the patience... and the diaper changing and the crying..." She shivers. "No thanks."

"I'm glad we're on the same page, wifey."

CELEBRATIONS

Sophie

I knock on the door of the computer room. "Twitch!"

He swivels his chair around to face me. "Yeah."

"If I email you this contract, can you print it for me?"

He frowns. "Give me your phone, and I'll add the printer to it. Then select the file and go to print and choose our printer."

That all went over my head, so I pass him my phone. "Here, can you do it?"

He starts working on my phone and then looks up and asks, "Are you coming tonight?"

I don't recall anything happening. "What's on tonight?"

"The fights at the warehouse."

It's not usually my thing, but I'll give most things a go. "I think I might. Do the other women go?"

"No."

His blunt response should be a red flag for me, but red flags seem to be my thing now. "Why not?"

"The violence… the blood… not their scene."

"Are you saying it's mine?" I question with a brow raise.

He shakes his head. "No," he says, backtracking.

I shift on my feet as the images of men violently fighting flash through my mind. "Is it safe?"

"You'll be safe there with Viper. Where's the contract located so I can print it?"

"It's already opened in my email… Aren't you going to the fights?"

"I don't really care. If Reaper wants me to stay here with the women, I will."

That piques my interest. "Why wouldn't you want to be with the men watching?"

"Watching men wrestle in a ring while other men yell at them"—his top lip rises—"Don't get me wrong, it pulls in money for us, but yeah, I'm happy to chill here, where I'm not choking on the smell of smoke, beer, and blood."

I crinkle my nose. "Oh, splendid," I say as the printer begins to run. I do get along with Twitch. He has waves of thick brown hair and a sprinkle of facial hair. I've never been attracted to men who wear jewelry, but his earring, leather bracelet, and rings suit him.

"What are you interested in then, Twitch?"

He casually shrugs. "Anything tech-related."

"Why?" I can't stop the distaste seeping into my tone.

"I enjoy learning and the challenge that comes with it."

I cackle, unable to hold it in. "You like a challenge? Is that why you like Milly?"

He shakes his head, but the corner of his mouth tips ever so slightly. These men and their games. I tut. "Were you in the military like the rest of them?"

"I didn't serve for long. I got medically discharged."

My shoulders fall. "I'm sorry to hear."

"It's fine." He turns, grabs the papers from the printer, and hands them to me.

"Can I borrow a pen?"

He hands me one from the desk.

"Thank you."

I take the contract and make my way to the dining room to read over it. I flick through the pages. It's reasonable. Dad's ensured that my assets—a mix of property, land, shares, and money I've inherited—stay with me if Viper and I go our separate ways.

My throat thickens. I push that thought to the back of my mind and sign the last page, hoping this will satisfy Dad, even though I know it won't.

Candy and Mercedez walk past. "Blondie, do you know where Viper is?"

They stop in their tracks. Mercedez's eyes widen. Candy's lips go into a hard line. "Shouldn't you know where he is?" she asks, dripping attitude.

I see her stalker eyes lurking after him, watching him all the time. "You sure you don't know?" I smirk.

"I think he's sparring with Rage, getting ready for tonight," Mercedez replies.

I grab the paper and pen off the table and make my way through the house and outside, where Viper is holding a large pad and Rage is punching it.

"Viper," I say and wait until Rage and Viper stop. "I need you to sign the contract for Dad."

"The one to ensure I don't touch your money?"

I give him a tight smile. "That's the one."

Without hesitation, he puts the pad on the ground, steps over to me, and grabs the pen. I go to pass him the contract, but he grasps only the last page, and signs it.

My shoulders fall an inch. Maybe there was a part of me that was worried that he did only marry me for my money.

"Will that be enough to appease your father?"

I wish. "I think you know the answer to that."

"Are you fighting tonight?" I ask Rage.

"Sure am."

"Bring on the money," Viper says in a playful voice while staring at Rage.

"I'm coming," I tell them.

Viper's brow slowly lifts. "Are you sure about that?"

I can't help myself. "Call me curious."

"Okay…" he says, his tone patronizing.

"Are you going to the gym this afternoon?" I ask Viper.

His lips curve up into a sexy grin. "I am if you are."

I smile back at him. I love how comfortable I am with Viper. He's easygoing and happy to go along with whatever I ask. I'm sure I'm not the easiest person to deal with.

"What do I wear tonight?" I ask, knowing I have to be practical. I can't just put on a dress and heels and walk into an illegal fight with God knows what people will be there.

"Jeans, shirt, enclosed shoes."

After we leave the gym, I'm flustered and aching with need from seeing Viper's arms flex when he lifted the weights, seeing how the sweat misted his skin during his workout and how the tank top showcased his rounded shoulders and corded pecs. The women followed him around the gym.

Once in the truck, I scan the parking lot. No one is around, and I'm suffocating with need. My eyes lock back onto Viper. His coconut-and-lime cologne and manly sweat are a potent combination. "I want you in me now," I murmur. His eyes widen, then darken. I go to pull down my shorts, but his hands hold mine firmly in place.

"We are in a parking lot. I'm not having men see you."

My inner slut curses at him. I don't care who sees us. All I know is I'm wet and blind with need. "Take me back to the clubhouse then. Hurry!"

We make it back in record time. The truck skids into the shed, and Viper parks it at a haphazard angle. I crawl into the back seat. Delicious anticipation fills me. I pull my shorts and thong down over my ass. "Come in the back seat with me," I say through heavy breaths.

Viper's scanning the shed. Though I saw no one out front when we drove in, the thought of someone catching us makes my stomach flutter. "No one's here," I reassure him.

He pauses. "Fucking hell, Sophie."

Internally, I'm cheering at the wavering resolve in his voice.

He gets out of the front seat and gets in the back with me. His eyes roam me thirstily, but I'm possessed. "Pull down your goddamn shorts, Viper!"

He gives me a small chuckle, and when he kicks off his shorts, his dick looks painfully hard. He leisurely strokes it a few times from the base to the head, which only urges me on further. I straddle him. Primitive instinct takes over my body.

He aligns us, and when I feel the crest of him pressing against me, he says, "Ride me, wifey," in a husky voice. I slowly glide down, inch by glorious inch.

A groan reverberates through his chest as a sigh of pleasure leaves my lips when I feel the fullness of him deep inside me. I lift and slowly lower again, feeling heat flooding through my body. The lust in his eyes and the need to fuck have me quickening the pace. There's movement in the corner of my eye, and when I peek to the side, I see Candy watching us. I give her a small smile, then focus back on Viper.

"Viper," I say, "you feel so good!"

The momentum is perfect as he rocks up to meet my drive. Our hearts pound, our chests heave for air, and our foreheads dampen with sweat. His hands are greedy, one cupping my heavy breasts through my sports bra, the other gripping my hair, pulling my mouth to his. Our tongues dance furiously as our rhythm becomes more desperate. Pleasure disperses with every plunge.

He's working harder and faster as we spiral out of control. "Fuck, Sophie!" he exclaims.

Everything tightens until ecstasy radiates from my core. As I go to scream, his mouth fuses to mine, swallowing my scream, and we ride out our orgasms together. I sink lax into his arms, sweaty and boneless as I try to gather air into my lungs.

"That was… wow…" he says through pants. I sit up, my eyes taking him in. I've always loved sex, but with him, I can't control myself. Hunger and primal need surge through me. My body constantly aches for his hands on my skin or his lips on mine and for us to be connected in the most intimate ways.

I glimpse to the side. Candy is no longer there. "Candy just watched us."

He shrugs, and the side of his lip quirks up. "Hopefully she's got the hint."

After a shower, I get changed, pulling my jeans up my thighs and wiggling into them, then doing up the zipper and button. I look up. Viper lies on the bed, relaxed, with his hands under his head and that cocky grin on his lips.

"What?" I ask.

"I'm here for the view. You have no idea how incredibly sexy you are. I can lie here and watch you get dressed over and over again."

Warmth floods my chest, and I give him a smile, but it's short-lived. "Crap! We were supposed to take the contract to Dad."

"It's okay, we will soon," he replies in a soothing voice.

I push that thought away. "What are we doing now?"

"The men are cooking a barbecue for dinner, and we're going to have a few celebratory drinks for Ava and Reaper. Then, later, the men will ensure the warehouse and everything are ready for tonight."

"How bad is it going to be?" I cringe when recalling Twitch's comments.

Viper stands and steps over to me. "You don't have to go. You can stay here."

My curiosity outweighs the reasons I should stay.

"Well… how about we just watch Rage's fight?" Viper asks.

I give him a sharp nod and follow his sexy ass out of the room, through the house, and out to the barbecue. Viper goes in the direction of the barbecue, while I veer off to the women sitting around the table.

"I can help," Ava says to the men by the barbecue.

"You're not cooking. Please sit down and relax," Reaper replies. He's standing next to Bomber and Viper, beer in hand.

Ava's lips purse. "Let me do a salad."

"No," Reaper says sternly. "The sweet butts have got it covered."

Ava shifts in her seat. I can see that she's dying to get up and help.

"Do you want me to make you a mocktail?" I offer as I take a seat next to Zara.

Ava gives me a kind smile. "Oh no, I've got my water, but thank you." Her skin is glowing. She was complaining about vomiting, but she looks great.

"Being pregnant looks good on you."

Ava sighs. "I feel terrible. I'm so bloated, and it's not morning sickness at all. The vomiting comes on at any time, day or night."

I'd like to uplift her mood. "When are we going baby shopping?" I ask.

Elena squeaks, doing a little side-to-side dance in her seat. The excitement is shining out of her.

Ava stares at the ground, a small frown on her face. "I want to err on the side of caution. So, not yet."

"How about we do just a small shop then?" Elena offers.

I cock my head. "Small shop" is not in my vocabulary, though I didn't promise it, Elena did.

Ava's shoulders drop. "Okay. Just a few clothes."

"Yes!" Elena cheers.

That gives me an idea, so while the women are talking, I move to the fire pit where Twitch, Axle, Cash, Rage, and Demon are sitting.

"How was the *truck ride*?" I don't miss the amusement dripping from Axle's tone.

"Were you watching as well?" I bite back in the same tone he used.

He lets out a loud laugh. "It's nice to have a woman around here who talks back."

The fact he likes having me around makes me smile. "How did you find out?"

"I overheard the sweet butts talking about it." Well, if Axle knows… everyone does. "Candy left by the way… She had some dodgy-ass friends pick her up."

"Left?" My voice falters. "For good or just for a while?" I want her gone for good, but at the same time, I don't want her involved with dangerous people.

"Well… she had all her bags. Mercedez tried to get her to stay, but Candy was determined to leave. The guy that got out of the car to help her with her bags was skinny and had scabs on his face and up his arms. He looked like he was a user."

A sliver of guilt tweaks my stomach. I try to shake off the feeling and think back to Ava's pregnancy.

"Hey, Twitch." I move close to him so that only he can

hear. "Can you do me a favor? If you have a copy of the War Brothers MC logo, can you send it to me? I want to put it on the back of a onesie as a surprise for Ava."

He waits a beat, then cocks his head. "What's a onesie?"

I grin. "A one-piece suit for babies."

He gives me a weird look. "Umm… Okay."

"The food is ready!" Bomber calls out, so I go back to the women around the table.

I hear them mentioning the charity. "That reminds me: I need to sort out my donation and call my brothers about theirs."

"You don't have to!" Zara is quick to respond.

"We want to," I reply in a reassuring tone.

She leans closer to me and whispers, "How are you and Viper?"

"Pretty amazing."

She smiles, obviously pleased with my answer. "He worships you."

So he should. An idea forms of how to get my husband back. I think he's the type that would love strippers, so a super-plus-size stripper it is. I grin and try to contain the excitement from bubbling up inside of me.

"Viper never felt anything for Candy."

"Axle was just telling me she left."

"Probably for the best… nice girl and all… but she would have wasted her time here because it seemed her world revolved around Viper, but he was never interested in her. He'd never be able to care for her the way he cares for or, I dare say, loves you."

My face drains of color. *Love*… I recoil as if I'm allergic to the word.

She laughs. "Don't make that face. I think he does… but before you faint, come and get some food."

I follow her in a daze. After we grab a plate, I sit down to eat, but her words have punched me in the chest.

Viper and I arrive at the warehouse near the edge of the MC's property. Loud cheering and yelling spill out from the opened doors. I swallow over the lump in my throat. My heart is pattering—I'm unsure what I'm going to walk in on. We meet Cash by the front entrance.

"How's Rage? Is he ready?" asks Viper.

"He's rearing to go," Cash responds, but waves of anxiety crash over me.

"Good, good," Viper replies. He peers over his shoulder at me and frowns. "We can go back to the clubhouse. You don't have to watch the fight."

He reads me well. Before, I wanted to sus out what it was, but now I'm not sure. The rowdy people and witnessing Rage get hurt aren't appealing, but this is what the MC does, and I'm not one to back down. I stand up straight. "You'll protect me, won't you?"

He offers me one of his panty-dropping grins. "I sure will, wifey."

I nod and grasp his hand. We step inside, and the smell immediately strikes me in the face. Twitch was right. Blood, sweat, smoke, and BO make my face morph in disgust. I swallow back the vomit and try to just breathe through my mouth.

I stand on my toes and look around. The ring is in the center of the warehouse, and a large crowd of men surrounds it on all sides. Two men leave the ring, blood running down their faces.

"Where do you want to watch it from? Do you want to go up to the front?" Viper asks.

Having to stand shoulder to shoulder with a rowdy crowd gives me the ick. "Here is just fine." Since the ring is raised, I'll still be able to see the fight, just not as clearly.

Viper tugs on my hand until we are at the outside perimeter of the crowd. He grabs my hips and pulls me in front of him. He's behind me, protecting me.

The lights dim, apart from one bright light aimed at the ring. Axle comes into view. "Gentlemen," he says into the microphone and the crowd quietens. "I hope you have placed your bets." I can taste the anticipation that's thick in the air.

"Now for the main event…" The crowd's volume intensifies, and the men huddle and push closer to the stage. "Here is Rage… the reigning champion."

I flinch at the roar of the crowd. Viper tightens his grip on me.

A heavy beat blares through the speakers as the singer screams the lyrics in a heavy metal song. The light darts to the left-hand side, where I can see movement. The crowd parts. My pulse speeds up.

I stand on my toes to get a look at him, but the music stops. Lights flood the warehouse. I blink a few times, feeling dazed. Everyone is looking around as well, seeming as confused as I am.

Reaper jumps up and into the ring, eyes wide with concern. "Everyone out," he barks. "The police are on their way."

Nervousness digs its nails into my chest while panic spreads like wildfire through the crowd. Immediately, Viper grabs my arm, pulling me along as everyone rushes toward the exits. I take one last look at the stage as icy-cold dread fills my stomach. I hope this isn't my father's doing.

FIFTEEN
LOVE-HATE

Sophie

I GOT LITTLE SLEEP. WORRY GRIPS ME TIGHTLY. THE MEN HAD A club meeting when we got home, and this morning, they were quieter. No one ended up in jail last night, which I'm thankful for, but the police were there to cause a scene. I guess the MC was lucky because the club's police contact tipped them off.

A horrible feeling crawls under my skin at the thought of jeopardizing the club and my relationship with Viper. Viper wouldn't confirm whether it was my father, so I hope to approach Dad this afternoon, after my day with the girls. This time I have the contract.

I shake my head and try not to let my thoughts put a negative vibe on today's excitement.

"They're so tiny," Zara says in a high-pitched voice, pulling out a small onesie with frogs on it.

"Are babies really that small?" I ask no one in particular.

"They sure are," Ava replies.

"So, what colors… white, yellow, and green is it?" Elena asks. "Since you're not finding out the sex."

"That's right," Ava answers.

Elena pulls out two sets of baby clothes and puts both in her hand before moving on to another row of clothes.

"You can only buy one piece of clothing," Ava warns.

Elena lets out a long groan. "One piece?"

Ava bobs her head. "*One* piece!"

"That's not fair! I'm the auntie—I should be allowed more."

Ava shakes her head, though she knows she can't stop us.

"It's okay, Elena. Me and you will be back in here shopping up a storm when she has the baby," I say with a wink.

Elena chuckles. "I'm down for that!"

But then I think, I won't be here when she has the baby. My heart constricts. I'm excited for Ava and Reaper, and even though I'm not a kid person, I'll be missing out on so much after I leave.

"Can we go get something to eat now? I'm feeling a little nauseous," Ava says.

I force a smile. "Sure." We briskly go to the checkouts.

We order food and drinks at the local diner and sit at a table outside.

"Remind me to get the back seat of the truck cleaned," I say. The women laugh, except for Ava, who smiles but averts her eyes. "Viper makes me so…" I fan my face. It was hot as hell.

"Do you know where Candy went?" I ask. "I must admit I feel a little bad about the man she left with."

"I don't know if she's left for good," says Elena.

Hoping I assumed wrong, I ask, "Did the men mention why the police turned up at the warehouse last night?"

Silence. Everyone's eyes are shooting to one another.

"I knew it! It was my dad, wasn't it?"

Elena's eyes drop to the ground. Ava gives me a tight smile, so I glance at Zara. She gives me a small nod.

"I need to talk to him." Even if the thought tightens my throat. "Do you mind if I leave soon? The whole incident has upset me, and I want to try and resolve it with Dad."

After lunch, the women go back to the clubhouse, but I get the family's chauffeur to pick me up. Once I take a seat in the limousine, I take my phone out of my bag and call Lawson.

"Hey," he answers.

"Hey, do you know where Dad is right now?"

"When I was talking to Alec this morning, he mentioned Dad was at home today."

"Thank you," I reply. "Do you still want to offer a donation to Zara's charity?"

"I do."

"Great. I'll call you later to get it sorted then."

"To my father's home," I say to the chauffeur.

When we pull up outside, I open the door and get out. The sun instantly warms my skin. I take a moment and gaze out at the calm lake and let out a long sigh before making my way past the guard and inside.

"Dad, where are you?" I call out before the door closes behind me. As I walk through the hallway, I hear his voice. He's standing in the living room, looking out at the lake while on his phone.

He turns, sees me, and nods in acknowledgment, so I take a seat.

My eyes latch onto a vintage whiskey decanter with two tumblers next to it. "Don't mind if I do," I mutter under my breath, knowing I'm going to need it. I pour a generous amount into the glass, bring it to my mouth, and shoot it back. I repeat the motion twice more, feeling the burn travel from my mouth to my stomach.

Once finished with his call, he walks to me and bends over

to kiss my cheek before taking a seat next to me. "How have you been?"

My lips press into a thin line. *I've been better, no thanks to you.* My body tingles with anxiety. I pull the contract from my bag and pass it to him. "This is what you wanted. Please stop causing problems with the MC."

He slowly takes the contract from me and flicks through it to the last page. He nods, then places it on the table. He says, "I'm surprised, but"—I sigh in disappointment; of course there's a but—"I want you to get a divorce. I want it all over and done with."

I peer down at my wedding ring and frown. "It's between me and Viper... no one else." I know I was planning on leaving after a month, but I'm faintly aware I'm not so sure what I want anymore. All I know is I don't want anyone else to make that decision for us.

"I wanted a better life for you. It's unsafe being with him. He's a biker... a thug... The club will always be his priority, and you will come second to that. I'm proving my point, causing disruption."

My eyes narrow at the arrogance in his voice.

"I've got people watching the clubhouse. If the MC tries to get that shipment through, I'll have people there to make that impossible, and every illegal fight they hold, I'll make sure cops are there for that too. You'll see... Viper will choose the club and end it with you."

I scowl. If anything, Viper has shown me he's willing to stand up to my dad, despite putting the club at risk. I keep it to myself, though my irritation festers.

"You can do better! Don't waste your life with a man in an MC."

"It's my decision!" We're both shocked at my outburst, but I can't keep holding everything in. It's not the MC's fault.

He pauses, then glares daggers. "Your little stunt in Vegas is an embarrassment to your family."

I recoil and gasp. He knows exactly where to stab the knife and make me bleed. I've tried to be successful and carve out my own career. I've worked so hard to prove to him I can run a successful business, and I make one choice he doesn't agree with, and it makes me *an embarrassment?*

"Are you giving up your business for him too?"

Horror widens my eyes. I would never be a woman who gives up her career for a man. *Is that what I'm doing right now?*

"No," I stammer as my heartbeat thumps in my ears. "I'm managing my business from the clubhouse, via phone calls and emails." I glance at his phone. "Just like you're probably doing."

The disbelief in his eyes irks me. I look away as heat rises through me.

"And if your business needs you in person?"

My chin rises. "I trust my employees—that's why I pay them the wages I do. But while I'm here, if my employees needed me in person, I'd go back to New York to see them."

I fold my arms across my chest, but my eyes water. I'm a grown-ass woman. I wish I didn't yearn for my dad's approval. I wanted to make my family proud and pave a way for myself. Just coming here and talking to him has made me doubt myself and stirred up inner turmoil about my priorities.

The thought of leaving Viper and my family and going back to New York makes me feel queasy. "I thought you'd be happy I'm back in Crown Village," I say, my voice choked with emotion.

"Of course I am." A sliver of lightness fills me until he says, "But not if you're making irresponsible and reckless decisions."

My body sags. I can't talk about this any longer. "I'm organizing a donation to Zara's charity, Misty's Safe Haven. Do you want to contribute to it as well?"

He inches back, a thoughtful look on his face. "Yes, it will be good publicity."

"I'm donating anonymously," I deadpan.

He frowns. "Why would you do that?"

My eyes drift around his face. I can understand my brother Alec, but how did Lawson, Harrison, and I come from him? I guess we went to private schools and then, when we came home, were raised by nannies. My father sees everything through a business lens. Lawson, Harrison, and I only want to help Zara support the charity. We don't need a pat on the back or to impress anyone.

"If you're donating publicly, you should talk to Zara. I'll speak to my brothers about their contributions. I'm going to get going." I add, "Please leave the MC alone." But I know he won't listen to me—he'll do what he wants.

I turn my back and dash out the door and into the limousine. "To the clubhouse," I tell the chauffeur. My muscles are screaming with tension. I blankly stare out the window, knowing I need to find a way to make Dad back off and allow me and Viper to decide what we want on our own, without his influence. To pull myself out of my funk, I call my brothers, who agree to make contributions to the charity.

Once I arrive at the clubhouse, I get out and go inside to see all the women in the kitchen. I take a seat on a stool at the kitchen island, across from Elena and Ava, who are peeling vegetables.

"Do you need any help?"

Ava smiles. "That's okay. With all of us here, we'll be finished soon."

I watch as she pulls a yam out of the container, and the veins, discolored skin, and shape make me laugh. When the women turn to me, I point to the yam in Ava's hands. "It looks like a dick."

Everyone's eyes lock onto the yam. Ava drops it on the table, making me laugh again.

"I got a dick pic, and no word of a lie—it resembled a yam, just like that one."

"That's hilarious," says Trixie.

"So wrong…" says Elena as her nose scrunches.

I sigh with a smile on my face.

"Tell me it wasn't Viper's," Mercedez says with a look of horror.

"Oh, good Lord, no." I think back to Viper's long, thick dick. "Viper's dick was crafted by the gods. That yam-dick photo was from a cop."

Elena's eyes bulge. "A cop sent you that?"

I nod. "He sure did."

I look around, but it's just us women. I don't remember seeing many bikes out front. "Where are all the men?"

"They went for a bike ride. They'll have lunch and a beer at the pub while they're out," says Elena.

Perfect timing. "Well… I'm thinking about getting my cocky, manipulative husband back." For all the cockblocking I had to endure, it's only fair.

Dolly bounces over to me with a big smile on her face. "What are your plans?"

"I'm thinking about organizing a bachelor party because Viper didn't have one before we got married. I'm going to tell him I got him a surprise so that he thinks it's going to be a normal stripper but…"—I wiggle my eyebrows—"I'm going to organize a super-plus-size stripper or wrestler. I haven't made up my mind yet."

The women cackle. Ava asks, "What did you just say?"

"I've heard about plus-size women strippers and wrestlers. I don't care if I have to pay to have the woman travel here. It will be worth it to see Viper's cocky smirk ripped from his face, and I think it will be hilarious." Not to mention I want everyone to have a laugh.

"So… I have an idea what the stripper does, but what exactly does a wrestler do?" Elena asks.

"She wrestles him… and, you know, throws him around a bit."

Elena giggles and slaps her leg. "Oh… it's going to be so funny." Her face falls. "But if it's a bachelor party, I gather we won't see it."

"I can just say that when Viper's surprise gets here, all the women are going out, and we can make a scene of getting up and pretending to leave, but when the stripper comes in, we'll stay and watch the show."

"Oh, good," Elena replies. "Because I don't want to miss it."

I go upstairs and into Viper's room, where I pick up my laptop from the bedside table and sit on the bed, crossing my legs. I type "plus-size stripper and wrestler" into the internet search bar and make a call to the best advertisement on Craigslist, then I check my work emails. After my daily call to the manager, I make a call to my accountant to check whether she has everything necessary to complete the month-end financials.

I'm tired from the lack of sleep last night, so I place my laptop off to the side and lie down. I take a deep breath; Viper's scent is on the pillows. His cologne smells divine. Tiredness weighs heavy on me, so I close my eyes and fall asleep.

There's a gentle tug on my shoulder. "Hmm…" I mumble.

"Sophie, it's dinnertime."

I slowly open my eyes, until Viper comes into view. He's standing by the bed, looking amused. "Come downstairs and have some dinner."

I roll onto my back and stretch out, yawning as I do. Viper bends and pokes his fingers into my side, making me jolt. He chuckles. "Get that sexy ass up and come eat while it's hot."

I grudgingly get up, though I stumble when I get to my feet. Viper's quick. His hands are firmly around my waist, holding me upright, making my heart race from his touch. He looks me over. "Are you okay?"

My skin flares beneath his hands. The warmth in his eyes and the concern in his voice make me lean into him, wrap my arms around his neck, give in to my body's demand, and bring his lips to mine. He hums in satisfaction and pulls me flush against him.

It's slow, soft, evocative, but it's the most intimate kiss. I'm drenched in him, savoring him, until he inches away, making me ache without his lips on mine. Every touch and every kiss make me crave more, but that kiss felt *different*. I pull out of his grasp, avoid eye contact, go downstairs, and try to ignore my fierce need for him.

After eating dinner and having a few drinks, everyone is out back. The music is loud, and the men and a few of the sweet butts are sitting around talking, away from the table on the sandstone blocks, while some of the men smoke cigars. The rest of us women are at the table, drinks in hand.

The women are talking around me. I peek over at Viper, and our eyes lock. He's been watching me closely all night. My emotions are all over the place. The kiss between us was intense. A shiver rolls down my spine. I'm becoming overly attached.

I've been causing all these problems with the MC, and it's eating at me. Maybe I should consider leaving and divorcing Viper. It's what's best for the MC.

"What's wrong with you tonight?" Zara asks from beside me.

I shake my head. "Dad's getting to me... that's all."

She puts her hand on my arm. "Try not to let it get to you. I'm sure it's just threats."

I need a distraction. On my phone, I go to messages. A slow smile spreads across my face as I type to Viper:

Viper

I need dick

I watch Viper glance down at his phone. His eyes widen, then he abruptly stands. With heat in his eyes, he gives me a sexy grin and struts over, so I stand to greet him. He interlocks his fingers with mine and gives me a hard kiss on the lips. "What wifey wants… wifey gets."

He pulls me away. After rushing upstairs and into the bedroom, he cradles my face in his hands. "I want you to know you can be a successful businesswoman and also be a wife. You don't have to choose one or the other."

My breath catches. I can't speak, so I nod. Then his lips meet mine, and I lose myself to him for the rest of the night.

SIXTEEN

BACHELOR PARTY

Sophie

RUN. BUSINESS. GYM. SEX. SOCIALIZING. SEX. *REPEAT.*

That's my routine with Viper. Days tick on by, and I can feel the anxiety building up inside me as I wait to see what Dad's next move will be.

I should just tell him I plan to leave when the month is up, but then I have to explain why, and I don't want another lecture about how stupid I was to agree to it in the first place. There's a tug-of-war between staying longer and going back to New York, so I grab my phone and call Piper.

"Hello," she answers.

"Hello, what have you been up to?"

She sighs. "I've been working long days this week. My boss has been really busy, so by the time I get home, I have a quick dinner and then crash and burn. How have you been with the big bad biker?"

I smile at her cheekiness. "Good, I've got the wrestler slash stripper coming tonight. Would you believe it: I found a woman who does both. I'm excited for it." *So* goddamn excited.

Piper lets out a loud laugh. "You're still going ahead with that?"

"I sure am. The limousine is picking her up and bringing her here." It's payback, even though I've started to find myself secretly thankful that Viper blackmailed me—not that I'd ever tell him that. I wanted to ease some of the tension in the clubhouse for one night, at least.

"Aww… I've missed you. It's been quiet without you here."

My heart swells. "I've missed you too."

"Well… call me tomorrow and tell me all about it," she says.

"I will… Bye."

I leave the room and go down the stairs. When I reach the bottom, I see Viper. "Can you get everyone together in the living room? I want to make an announcement."

His brows furrow. "What about?"

"It's a surprise," I say through a smile. "Go on," I say, shooing him away. I watch him swagger outside and sigh—my husband is sexy.

I go to the living room, where Twitch, Elena, Ava, and the sweet butts are watching TV. "It's time to announce Viper's surprise," I say to the women and add two winks at the end. They giggle.

"What surprise?" Twitch asks.

"It's a secret, sorry," I'm quick to reply so that the women don't tell him.

"Who knows?" he asks accusingly.

"Only us women know," I answer him.

The men trickle in, giving me interested stares as they settle around the room. Axle takes a seat beside Elena, Reaper beside Ava, and Bomber beside Zara.

Viper comes in and stands by me. "Is this everyone?" I ask him.

"Yeah," he answers after a few seconds.

I clap my hands and smile broadly as I look around. "So, since my hubby"—I peek at Viper—"didn't get a proper bachelor party, like the good wife I am, I've decided to organize one for him, and I've got a special surprise in store."

There's a round of deep cheers. Elena and Ava look like they might combust as they barely contain their laughter. Viper wraps an arm around me. "Wifey, you didn't have to do that," he coos.

"Oh, I did," I say in a fake caring tone.

"When's the *surprise* coming?" Axle calls out.

"The bachelor party is tonight, so if you have plans, cancel them. And yes, tonight is when the surprise will be coming."

Judging by the wide smiles on the single men's faces, they're ecstatic about my idea.

When everyone disperses, I move to the couples.

"I thought you'd be upset," Axle says to Elena.

She puts a hand on his leg. "I just want Viper to have a *good* night."

Axle kisses her cheek. "Wow… thanks, babe… for being so understanding."

"It's okay," she replies in a cheerful voice.

"Are you staying?" Bomber asks Zara.

"No, us women will leave when Viper's surprise arrives."

Bomber frowns. "I'll go with you. I don't want to watch a stripper."

Zara looks away, like she's trying to suppress her laughter. "Trust me…" she replies, "you want to be here for it."

He tilts his head and studies her face, so I subtly catch her attention and put a finger to my lips. She better not tell him! Bomber's eyes glance between all of us.

Viper leans into me. "I know it's a stripper. You don't have to pretend it's a secret."

I peer at him and bat my eyelashes, then lower my voice to a whisper. "You're not supposed to know."

He pulls me closer to him and whispers back, "You can cancel her. I'd be happy getting a private show from you."

"Oh well... I've already organized and paid for her travel here. I wanted to get you the best." And the best he shall get.

Rage walks over to us. "Do any of you want to put in an order for drinks? We're low on a few things, so I'll go down now and grab some for tonight."

"I wouldn't mind grabbing some more cocktail ingredients," I reply.

"I'll come with you," Viper says.

The three of us take the truck to town. Viper hops in the driver's seat, I get into the passenger seat, and Rage gets in the back. At the store, Rage grabs a cart, and we walk through the aisles. In the walk-in cooler, I shiver as the air bites my skin, and I break out in goosebumps. Rage and Viper grab cases of beer and place them in the cart. Next, we shop for spirits. There's so many to choose from. I pull out a bottle of peach schnapps and a bottle of apple vodka for Jolly Rancher shots, and standard vodka and triple sec for kamikaze shots. I pause, thinking about what cocktails the girls will like.

"I thought you weren't staying tonight?" Rage asks and laughs.

I slowly turn my head to him. "I want to make sure there's plenty available so that when I want to make drinks, all the ingredients are there."

"Cocktails, cocktails..." I mutter to myself. Hmm... piña coladas and cosmos. I grab a bottle of Cointreau and put it into the cart. "What else do we need?" I ask Viper and Rage.

"Whiskey and wine," Rage replies.

After getting the remaining cocktail ingredients, we pay

and walk outside to the truck, where Viper and Rage place the drinks in the back.

An odd shudder travels down my spine. I sense someone watching me. I survey the parking lot, but I can't see anyone watching me. I could be paranoid… or it could be one of Dad's employees keeping tabs on me.

The back door shuts, making me jump. "Are you all right?" Viper asks.

I give him a tight smile. "I'm fine, let's go back to the clubhouse."

As we pull out and accelerate slowly, we pass groups of people smoking. One looks like Candy. I turn to look over my shoulder, but her back is to us. The resemblance is uncanny.

My phone rings. When I look at the screen, it's a number I don't recognize.

"Hello, Sophie speaking."

"Hi, it's Gina. I just got picked up in a luxurious limousine and I'm on my way."

Giddy excitement bubbles up inside me. "That's fabulous." I beam. "Enjoy the free wine and food."

She squeals. "I will. I think it's going to take a couple of hours to get there."

I look at Viper, who's glancing at me every few moments. He leans over as if trying to listen to our conversation.

"Well… you rest up. You're going to have a night full of activity."

"Is he ready for me?" she asks in a low voice.

I hold back a laugh and stare at Viper as I say, "Oh… he's ready for you."

Viper's eyes light up, and I take deep breaths as I try my best to maintain my composure.

That night after dinner, I encourage the men to have a few beers while they wait for the show. Ava, Elena, and I rearrange the living area. I drag over some chairs from the dining room and arrange them in a circle for the men, with one chair in the center for Viper.

Axle is leaning against the wall, watching us. "Since we already know it's a stripper, are we getting A-plus top-notch material or B-grade inexperienced?"

"A-plus grade," I reply, while Elena snorts.

Axle's smile grows wider. "You're such a cool chick." Then he looks at Elena. "And thanks again, babe."

"No trouble at all," Elena answers.

His face falls. "Are you sure it's okay? Is this the type of thing where you're saying you're okay, but once it's over you're going to be pissed at me… Or is it a challenge? Have I failed?"

She shrugs nonchalantly, but the corner of her mouth twitches. "Not at all. I just want Viper to have a good night."

After everything is set up, I set the mood and put on some sensual music. There's a happy vibe among the crowd. All the couples are at the bar having a drink while others are talking amongst themselves. I bite back a laugh at the broad smiles on Axle's, Twitch's, and Rage's faces. They are going to be pleasantly surprised at what I have in store for them.

"Oh," I turn to Viper. "I need to blindfold you for the surprise. What can I use?"

"I have my bandana for the Harley upstairs. It's in the bedside table's drawer."

"Is that the one with the snake on it?" I ask.

He nods. I've seen it before; he uses it to cover his nose and mouth when he rides on the motorcycle at times.

My phone beeps. I pull it out to see a message saying, "I'm here."

Buzzing energy flows through my body. "She's here!" I yell out. "Twitch, can you open the gate for the limousine?"

"I can do that," he says, smiling.

"Ava, do you mind going into Viper's room and grabbing

his bandana from the drawer of the bedside table and putting it on him, covering his eyes?"

Then my gaze shifts to Zara. "Can you let me know when the bandana is on because I don't want Viper to see her until after he takes the blindfold off?"

"I'll go now," Ava says and goes up the stairs.

"Men, take a seat," I say. The women stand and pretend to leave but move out of the room to where they can still see the men in their chairs. Everyone is smiling, and I can't say who looks more excited, the men or the women.

I rush to the front door as Gina's stepping out of the car. She's six feet and around four hundred pounds. This is going to be some good entertainment. She's wearing a snug dress with a bikini top underneath.

When I reach the limousine, I say, "Hi, Gina. I'm Sophie. Thank you for coming."

She looks me over. "Aren't you a pretty little thing?" she says with a smile. "The wine and food went down a treat. Is this the place?" She peers at the clubhouse.

"It sure is. Viper's inside… my friend is putting a blindfold on him… to surprise him."

"He doesn't know I'm coming?" she asks mischievously.

"He doesn't. He thinks I've hired, you know…"—I bite my bottom lip, not wanting to offend her—"a standard stripper."

She chuckles evilly. "Even better."

"He's ready," Zara says and waves to Gina.

As we walk to the front door, Gina asks, "What do the men do here?"

"It's a motorcycle club."

Her eyes light up. "Oh… I've got myself some sexy bikers."

I lead her inside. "Music!" I yell out. Twitch puts on my requested song, "Sexy Bitch" by David Guetta and Akon.

Gina sashays her hips to the beat. As we walk through the house, my heart beats faster, and when we reach the living room, the crowd takes a collective gasp.

Axle yells, "What the fuck…" as the women giggle off to the side.

Everyone's eyes are bulging as the stripper grabs her dress and literally rips it in half, throwing the shredded material to the floor, showcasing her red bikini top and bottoms. Viper, still blindfolded, rubs his hands together and licks his lips.

Gina sensually moves her hips to the music, then turns and twerks, giving the men a good view. There's a mix of cheers and shock throughout the crowd. She shimmies her hips, taking one slow step after another toward Viper. She lifts one leg and plops onto his lap, straddling him. His face drops.

"Hey, sugar, I'll take your blindfold off for you," she says seductively. When she pulls it off his eyes, he pales, and I burst out laughing.

Gina pulls Viper's head between her ginormous breasts and shimmies her shoulders, motorboating him. The laughter that erupts around the room is loud. The men are pointing and rolling around in their chairs.

Gina slowly gets off Viper, and his little face appears. He grimaces and pulls away from her. As soon as she steps away from him, he bounces off the chair and tries to get out between Demon and Bomber, but they block him.

He tries again, between Rage and Twitch, but they stand, not letting him out either. Gina prances further away from Viper, in the opposite direction, which confuses the crowd. When she turns around, her face is set in a determined scowl. She charges at Viper, her body bouncing from side to side with each stride, as she yells, "Rahhhh!"

Rage and Twitch push Viper back into the middle of the circle again. Viper closes his eyes, probably praying to God, then, *SMACK*, she tackles him to the ground. The crowd erupts as the men stand, cheer, and holler.

Viper's on his back, though I can see only his legs kicking. I hold my stomach as I laugh. Tears trickle down my face.

She sits up, grabs his hands, and rubs them on herself. "How do you like that, precious?" she purrs.

He has to move some of her stomach roll out of his face to talk. "Help me!" he yelps.

The slight fear in his eyes only makes me laugh harder. My stomach aches, and I'm gasping for air.

Gina wiggles down Viper's body, her stomach and thighs sweeping, touching him as she puts her arm out to get up onto her knees. Reaper leans down and helps her to her feet while Viper looks paralyzed.

"Help him up, boys," she says, then winks at them.

Reaper and Bomber bend down and pull Viper up. He stands, his eyes wide. He blinks and wipes the sweat, which is probably a mix of hers and his, from his forehead with his arm. They sit him back down in the chair.

She dances, doing body rolls and shimmying her hips. She twirls around him, her arm trailing over his chest, the back of the chair as she circles him, then to his chest again when she reaches the front.

Gina turns around and backs her ass up until it's up near his face. "Oh, hell no!" he shouts as she twerks. He tries to back away, but he can't go anywhere. He pushes her booty cheeks away from him, pulling his head as far away from her as possible.

Everyone's in hysterics. "Tell her to stop!" he yells out, so I decide to give in before she suffocates him.

"Gina," I call out as I move toward them. I put my hand out and grasp hers. "Gina, everyone," I say and raise her arm up in the air as everyone cheers and claps for her performance.

Viper gets up and wipes his face again. "I can't believe that just happened," he murmurs, then shakes his head. After a moment, a small smile curves his lips. I breathe a little easier knowing he isn't angry at me. Instead, he steps over to Gina and shakes her hand.

Viper moves to me. "You are something, you know that."

I smile up at him. "We're even now. Just remember this… when you think about blackmailing or cockblocking me again."

He leans in close and lowers his voice so that only I can hear. "I'm going to have a shower."

When he leaves, I turn back to Gina. "You're welcome to stay for a few drinks if you like. I've organized a night's stay at the resort for you."

Gina peers around, her greedy eyes roaming the men. She licks her lips. "I think I'll stay for a few."

"Would you like a drink?" I offer.

"Just a beer, thanks."

I go to the bar fridge and grab her one, people patting my back and telling me how awesome that was as I move through the crowd.

I look around for Gina, but she's already on the dance floor. To one side, Axle is dancing with her, their backs together as they shimmy, while Elena and Ava are smiling at them. Axle's obviously gotten over his initial shock. To Gina's other side Dolly and Trixie, the sweet butts, are grooving with her. I smile wide, loving the carefree lifestyle of the MC.

SEVENTEEN
A WOMAN'S REVENGE

Sophie

After breakfast, the men leave for a meeting with their buyer.

"Didn't Viper go for a run this morning?" Elena asks with a smile.

"No… he did not." I laugh. "He was sore this morning… hobbling around. I think the tackle might have pulled a muscle or something."

Zara snorts. "Honestly, I haven't laughed so hard in ages. He feared for his life." She cackles. "I never want to forget that. It's going to live in my head rent free. What did he say about it? He didn't appear angry."

"Once he got over the shock, he knew it was for a bit of fun and payback. Not long afterward, he was laughing about it. The men are roasting him. What are you up to today?"

"I'm heading to the charity," Zara replies.

"I've got class," says Ava.

"I'll stay here and get on top of the washing," Elena says.

Ava looks at Elena. "Can you please wash Conan?"

Elena groans. "I'm going to get soaking wet… and smell like dog… but okay, I'll do it."

"What about you? What are you up to?" Zara asks me.

"I've got a few business items to attend to, then the gym. I'm considering going to see Dad at some point." I hate the conflict between my family, but I'm torn and don't know what to do.

Zara flinches. "Good luck."

I let out a heavy sigh. "Yes, I know… I'll need it."

Once I've finished with my work calls, I get changed into my shorts and crop top, put on my Nikes, and pull my hair back into a ponytail. I pick up my phone, pressing on the home screen. No phone calls or messages from Viper. My fingers itch to contact him, but I resist. I need to get a hold of myself.

I call the chauffeur and ask him to take me into town, then go out front and wait for him. I'm sitting on the porch when I hear the rumble of motorcycles. When I stand, they're coming closer, kicking up dirt as they go. The closer they get, the louder the bikes' engines become. When they come up the driveway, I see they're all wearing bandanas that cover their faces. They park in the shed.

My pulse races as Viper takes his helmet off and swings his leg over the bike. He gives me one of his sexy smiles as I rush to him. He pulls me into his arms and twirls me around as I squeal. Once he lets go of me, he grunts and grabs his back.

"Sorry…" I say through a laugh. "I forgot you were sore."

"That's okay." His eyes drift over me, coming to rest on my butt. "And where do you think you're going?" he asks, then smacks my ass.

I jump slightly. "To the gym."

"I'm coming," he's quick to answer.

With my hand on my hip, I ask, "How are you going to go while you're injured?"

"I can watch," he purrs.

I suppress a grin.

"What?" he asks coyly. "I like the view."

"I'm sure it's got nothing to do with giving men the evil eye when they check me out."

"I don't know where you got that idea from," he muses.

The limousine appears and accelerates slowly toward the house. "Well, my ride's here. Are you sure you want to come?"

He nods. "Sure am."

On the ride over, I ask, "Have the men been roasting you about last night?" Though I know the answer.

He groans. "Yes, they have… thanks for that."

I beam. "No worries."

He shakes his head at me, with his lip tilted up.

I consider telling Viper I'm going to see Dad soon, but I caused him enough grief last night, so I let it go.

"Have I convinced you to stay with me yet?" he asks. His voice sounds carefree, but there's a softness and vulnerability in his eyes. It feels like we're offering our hearts up to each other and greedily accepting while knowing our relationship will end in heartache if Dad keeps threatening the club.

I pause, my throat tightening. He gives me a sad smile and squeezes my thigh, and I rest my head on his shoulder. I never thought I'd fall for a guy so quickly and so hard. It goes against everything I've tried to ensure never happened, but Viper forced his way into my life. Now I don't know if I'll ever get out from under his spell.

My mouth parts to tell him I'm not sure if I want to go back to New York… that I'm considering staying to see where this leads, but I force my mouth closed. None of that matters if my father is adamant about threatening the MC.

After the gym, we have dinner and hang out with the rest of the MC. I sit on Viper's lap and listen to small talk. Contentedness and relaxation sink all the way to my bones.

We have an early night. I pull the sheets back and get into bed. Viper gets in beside me and moans, briefly closing his eyes, snuggling into the covers. "These sheets are like silk against my skin."

"I told you they're good. Actually, they're better than good…" I sigh. "They're amazing."

He turns to face me. "You've changed my life. You make everything better."

I go to speak, but his mouth captures mine in a slow, sensual kiss. Every day our bond grows stronger. When it's just us, our relationship is easy… like breathing.

"I've fallen in love with you," he murmurs against my lips.

My heartbeat spikes. "Shhh…" I reply, struggling to hold it together as I bury those feelings deep down.

"I want you… no, I need you to stay." I help him pull off his shirt, and he kicks off his briefs as I grab the hem of my nighty and pull it over my head. His body is a work of art. Skin stretched over corded lean muscle.

We reach for each other, unable to stop ourselves. I caress his warm chest and the hard planes of his body as he cups my breast and masterfully uses the pad of his thumb to circle my nipple.

He gets up and lies on top of me. I sigh at the weight and heat of his body as he cages me in. His eyes sear into mine. The moment feels like a lifetime, as if he's looking into my soul.

A myriad of emotions crosses his face before his lips take mine again, just as softly and tenderly as before. My legs circle his hips as he slowly pushes inside of me, making both of us moan.

"You were made for me," he whispers as he moves inside of me again.

I try to kiss him harder as my fingernails dig into him, but he shakes his head at me. He knows what I'm doing: trying to fuck and not be intimate. I'm overwhelmed with fear of what the future may hold, but his lips meet mine again, and he makes love to me.

When I wake up, our legs are tangled in a mess of bedsheets. Last night has me reeling. I need to speak to my dad about Viper. I need him to let us make our own decisions about our future.

After breakfast, I put on jeans and a shirt. "I'm going to see my dad this morning," I say to Viper.

He pauses. "Do you want me to come?"

"No, I think it will be best if I go by myself."

"Well… Do you want a lift? I've got to go into town anyway. I said I'd help Zara install some furniture and other bits and pieces she needs done at the charity."

I smile at him, proud that the MC is involved in something so selfless. "That would be great. Can we stop off at the store? I wanted to get a few more drinks. Everyone seems to enjoy the shots and cocktails I've been making."

He kisses the top of my head, and when he inches back, he grins. "That's because you make them taste so good."

When we park outside the liquor store, a group of people are hanging around outside, out back of an old run-down house. "Why do people hang around there?" I ask. The people are standing around smoking. They're rough-looking, with unkempt hair and clothes. I take a step closer to Viper.

"That house is a drug den. We don't have many users in town, but that place is where they hang out."

I frown. "That's sad. I didn't know there were any drug houses in Crown Village."

"Every town's got at least one. It's easy for them being in the house right next to the liquor store. That's actually where we got the dog, Conan, from. He was tied outside with no water or food, so Ava saved him."

Viper's phone rings. He gets it from his pocket and answers it. His face goes from happy to stern. "Okay, I'm leaving now," he says before putting his phone away.

"Look, I've got to go. There's a family that needs to be rescued urgently, and since I'm already in town, I can get there the quickest."

My stomach drops. I lean in and give him a peck on the lips. "Be safe."

"I will. Will you be okay getting a lift to your dad's?"

"I'll get the chauffeur to pick me up, so don't worry about me. You go."

He nods, and the motorcycle revs as he races out of the parking lot.

After the cashier places the two bottles of liquor in the bag, I pay her and leave. Outside, I pull out my phone. "Hi, it's Sophie. Can you pick me up from the liquor store in town and take me to wherever my father is?"

"I'm on my way," the chauffeur answers. "I'll be twenty minutes."

"Thank you," I say and put my phone back in my pocket.

I hear a whistle and a round of laughter coming from the group of people outside the house. I inwardly groan and don't acknowledge them; instead, I look at the ground and pretend I don't hear them making vulgar comments. The sense of them getting closer makes me raise my head. It's

Candy, followed by two guys and a woman. I knew I saw Candy outside that day.

My pulse races as I glance back at the doors to the store. I have a knot in my stomach when I think of Candy moving out because of me and ending up here. When I see her up close, the guilt hits me hard. She's skinnier now, with deep hollow eyes and sores on her skin. She must have hit the drugs. When she reaches me, she searches around me.

"Are you okay? Do you need some help?" I ask her.

She laughs, so I take a step back while cautiously looking at her friends as they circle around me. My heartbeat is frantic as worry cloaks me.

"What… you care about me now?" Candy asks while scratching her arm. She points a finger at my chest. "You took away the one thing I had… I was going to be Viper's ol' lady until you turned up." Her voice is a mix of anger and hurt.

The bag is ripped from my hand. "What's this?" a man asks. I turn to him as he looks in the bag. "Score! These are mine now."

I gulp. "You can have them." I clear my throat. "My ride will be here soon," I say while trying to step between the man and the woman.

The woman pushes me back. Her feral eyes are on me. "So, this is the bitch that took your man?" she asks. Candy nods, frowning.

My breath is uneven and deafening in my ears. I urgently look around, searching for the limousine.

"This is payback," her friend says, right before she punches me in the face. Pain radiates, and the force pushes me back into the guys behind me, who throw me to the ground. My body hits the ground hard. A scream tears from my mouth.

Fists rain down on me. Pain ricochets through me. I squeeze my eyes shut and curl into a ball, instinctively covering my face with my arms. Then it's kicks from different angles, to my head, stomach, legs, and back. Punishing blow after blow. "We better go before the cops show up," a man says.

I force my swollen eyes open. Spit lands on me. When they run away, I gasp for air. I can taste blood, and I feel wetness over me.

The sound of footsteps comes closer, and relief floods me that someone is here to help. A woman's head comes into view. "Oh my," she chokes out, frowning. "Quick, someone call an ambulance!" she yells.

"Who did this?" a man asks.

"I saw a group of people running away from her." She peers back down at me, gently patting me. "We're going to get you some help, honey. The ambulance won't be long."

Everything blurs as I attempt to open my eyes. I'm struggling. The sirens wail in the background. At least the strangers saw me and called for help. The pain is overwhelming, and tears fall, stinging as they glide past the cuts on my face.

The ambulance arrives. When the paramedics roll me onto the stretcher, shooting pain fires through me, especially my ribs. As they wheel me away, the air nips at my sores, and the last thing I see is the roof of the ambulance before I lose consciousness.

EIGHTEEN

GUILT GUTS ME

Viper

I PULL INTO THEIR STREET AND AS I GET TO THEIR HOME, THE curtain moves. The coward comes running out and jumps in his car before I can park my bike. He tears out of their driveway, and the car's tires screech as he takes off.

I'm in Pearl Bay, the town next to ours, where there's more domestic violence. It always churns my gut. Every time I've turned up to escort a woman and her children to safety, I have to stop myself from beating the scum that laid a hand on them. It's painful, but we try to focus on the victims. We don't want to scare them with more violence, but it isn't without some serious self-control.

I knock on the front door, which is already open wide. "Hello." I take two steps inside. "He's gone. You called the Misty's Safe Haven hotline. I'm here to help you." There's no response, so I walk down the hallway. "I have the Safe Haven ID here in my wallet if you want to check."

A door to my left clicks, and the handle moves. A woman

opens the door an inch and peeps through. I pull my wallet out of my pocket, slide the ID out of the card section, and show it to her. "See, it's safe," I say in a reassuring tone.

Her eyes go to my ID, to my face, and back again. She slowly steps out so I can see her. She has a bruised eye and purple bruises around the nape of her neck. Tears stream down her face. "Thank you," she sobs. "Lucas," she calls out. "You can come out." A young boy dashes to her and wraps his arms around her legs, and it tears me to shreds to see a kid so scared.

I was bounced from one foster home to the next, and I remember feeling scared. I never felt safe during those early years.

My phone rings, so I pull it out and bring it to my ear. "Zara."

"Hi, Viper. How did it go? Are they safe?" she asks in a rush of words.

"They are."

She blows out a breath. "Tell them to pack their belongings and I'll be there soon."

"Will do."

"Thanks, Viper," she says before the call is disconnected.

My attention goes back to the woman and child. "Can you pack your bags? The people at the Safe Haven will be here soon to pick you two up."

She nibbles on her lip. "Can't we stay here?"

I shake my head with a sad smile. "It's not safe. He'll be back."

She bobs her head and turns, holding her child's hand.

Twenty minutes later, they walk out with their luggage and sit on the porch while I wait by my bike. Zara pulls up in the new truck she purchased with the money Sophie's family donated so that she can transport families from their homes to the charity.

I peer back at the mother and child. "Your ride's here."

The woman nods. "Thank you."

As Zara gets out and slowly walks to them, my phone rings—it's Bomber.

"Hey."

"Meet me at the hospital." He speaks fast, his voice stern.

Instantly my heart races and I briefly close my eyes. "Who is it?" I ask, fear softening my voice.

"It's Sophie."

I struggle to draw air into my lungs, like someone's gripping my throat. I jump on my bike, pull the throttle back, and speed through the streets, feeling the rush of air on my face. All I can think is Sophie has to be okay… she just has to be.

By the time I reach the local hospital, Bomber is standing outside waiting for me. When I get up close to him, the sadness in his eyes levels me.

"What happened?"

He frowns. "She was beaten up."

My hands clench by my sides. Anger and sadness twist at my insides. "Who the fuck would hurt her in this town, knowing who her family is and her connection with us? Once I find out who it was…" I chuckle darkly, wanting to cause pain to whoever hurt her, but right this minute, I have to be with her.

He pats my back. "I know, brother. When Milly realized who her patient was, she called me because I'm family, so let's go inside and see how Sophie is."

We make our way to the lobby, where a nurse sits at the reception desk. Bomber talks to her while my chest gets heavy as thoughts of what could have happened play through my mind.

I drag my hands down my face as I curse myself. I should've stayed with her. Someone else could have gone to the woman and child. Sophie's my wife, and I carelessly left her at the store.

Milly enters the lobby, and I rush to her. A frown mars her face.

"Tell me, is she okay?" Dread washes over me as I impatiently wait for an answer. Every second feels like a lifetime.

"We've done some scans and checked her out. She has a concussion and a few fractured ribs, and many superficial injuries. She also has some internal bleeding in her abdomen. If that doesn't resolve, she'll require surgery, so I want to keep her overnight to monitor her."

I search the corridor. "Where is she?"

She gives me a sad smile and my stomach drops. "I'm sorry, she doesn't want any friends or family seeing her yet."

My heart is beating like crazy. I run a hand through my hair. "I need to see her. Milly, I mean it—I'll search every room in this hospital until I find her." I know Milly is Reaper's sister and I don't mean to sound disrespectful, but I'm desperate to see Sophie. She needs me and is just being her stubborn self.

Milly's eyes soften with sympathy. "Viper, I'm your friend, but right now I am Sophie's doctor and she's my patient. If she doesn't want visitors, I won't let anyone see her." She folds her arms over her chest and her eyes narrow. "Don't make me get security and force you out of the building."

My jaw tightens. I like Milly, but right now, I dislike her. "When can I see Sophie?"

Milly's shoulders fall. "I'll talk to her and say that you're here."

I give her a sharp nod. "Tell her I'm not leaving until I see her."

I hear a man yelling and turn to see Garrett and Sophie's brothers by the reception desk. If Sophie sees her family before me, knowing I'm here, it's going to slice me open.

Lawson's eyes lock onto us and he rushes over, his brothers and Garrett close behind. "Where is she? Have you seen her? Is she okay?" Lawson asks.

I don't even have time to answer because Garrett is at our side and asks, "Are you her doctor?" as he peers at Milly.

"I am. Are you family?" she asks in a professional tone.

He nods sharply. "I'm her father." Then he looks at his sons. "And they are her brothers." All have deep frowns on their faces.

"Sophie was involved in a physical altercation. She has a concussion, fractured ribs, internal bleeding, and bruises and cuts on her body from being hit."

"Hit?" Garrett roars, making Milly jerk back. He turns to me and grabs me by the top of my cut. I shove him off me, resisting the urge to punch him once and for all. Alec and Harrison grab their father, and Bomber's arms come around me, pulling me backward.

"If this has anything to do with you, God help you and your fucking club." There is no mistaking the hatred in his voice, but I feel it too for the person who did this.

Adrenaline soars through me. "Don't you ever touch me again, old man!"

Bomber pulls me further away and says, "Let's take a walk." I shove him off me, feeling constricted, like the walls are closing in. My fists clench and unclench. It's like I'm going to explode. I hate feeling this out of control. We move to the waiting area, where I pace back and forth. Bomber stands by me.

"You hear that prick?" I ask Bomber. "Blaming me? Everyone I know loves Sophie. No one would hurt her." I stop pacing, thinking back to the people Sophie sounded wary of who were out at the back of the drug house.

"What's wrong?" Bomber asks.

I shake my head and rub my chest where it burns. "It

could have been the group that was hanging around at that shack next to the store. They could have beaten her for the booze she bought… I shouldn't have left her," I say through gritted teeth.

Bomber grips my shoulder. "Regardless of who did it, it's not your fault."

Lawson and Harrison make their way over and take a seat next to us. "Sorry about that," Harrison says. "Dad's worried about her… We all are."

Even though Garrett blamed me, his daughter is hurt, and if I had a daughter who was injured, I'd be stressing out too. "Don't sweat it," I reply.

Two police officers walk in, speak to the receptionist, and then walk past the lobby and toward where Garrett and Alec are standing. They talk to Garrett, nodding their heads, before going toward the hospital rooms, most likely where Sophie is.

"If you find out what happened before us, can you keep us updated?" Bomber asks his cousins.

"Sure," Lawson replies.

My eyes keep glancing at the clock on the wall, then down the white corridor with endless doors. Time feels like it's going so slowly. One hour rolls by, and I don't stop fidgeting until I see Milly's face again. She walks toward us, and everyone stands.

Milly looks at me. "You can come in now." I let out a heavy breath.

"What about us?" Lawson asks.

"Viper first," she answers him.

I follow her, but as I go past Alec and Garrett, Garrett follows us. Milly stops and looks at him. "Sophie wants to see Viper first."

He glares at her, so I move in front of Milly. "Watch what you say," I warn. I'm not having him try to scare Milly.

Milly taps me on the shoulder and sighs. "Let him come."

Her tone is soft. "Sophie was going to see him next anyway." Keeping him away from Sophie might be more trouble than it's worth.

With each step, my breathing becomes more panicky. We pass door after door until Milly pauses, enters a room, and pulls back a curtain. When my eyes land on Sophie, my knees buckle. Her face is covered with dark purple bruises, and both eyes are swollen. She can open only her right eye. Her hair looks matted. The sheet covers her from the waist down, but her arms are dotted with small bandages.

My legs are weak as I go around the bed and take a seat. All I want to do is hold her in my arms, but I'm scared I'll hurt her.

"What happened?" Garrett asks softly, which makes me peer back at him. He's standing at the foot of the bed, looking pale.

"Not now," Sophie replies, her voice hoarse.

Her hand folds over mine. I raise it only a few inches and lower my head to kiss the top of it. She gives me a sad smile, squeezes my hand, and closes her eyes. A moment later, her breathing evens out and she falls asleep.

"Is she okay?" Garrett asks Milly.

"The pain medication causes drowsiness. She's exhausted, and her body is trying to heal. Can you two wait in the lobby so she can rest?"

I want to argue. I want to stay with her. But I know she needs rest, so I follow Garrett out. "Did you find out who did it?" I cautiously ask him as we make our way towards the waiting room.

"The police said a bystander saw a group of young adults run away from her outside the store."

Suddenly, I'm in a chokehold and I can't breathe. *I left her, this is my fault.*

"Where were you?" Garrett asks, hurt and anger filtering

through. "Where were you when my daughter was being beaten?" he asks again, raising his voice.

Not with her where I should have been. "I'll find who it was."

The silence is tense. "I'm searching for them too, but if you find them first, you give them hell… it's the least you could do."

A storm is raging inside of me. "I'm going right fucking now."

He searches my eyes, then nods. "Don't let them get away with this." His voice holds a brutal edge.

I'm usually not a violent person, but if someone hurts the people I love, it changes everything. "I'll make sure to give them the message."

I meet Bomber and tilt my head to the exit. "We've got someone to visit."

NINETEEN
A HEAVY BURDEN TO CARRY

Viper

Bang! The door flies open, hitting the wall from the force of my boot. Even in daylight, the house is dark because newspapers cover the windows. The stench of shit, piss, and rotten food smashes me in the face. I gag, then quickly bring my bandana up to cover my nose and mouth. "That's fucking disgusting," I mutter, trying my best not to gag again.

As I step in further, with Bomber close behind, I hear, "Who the hell is that?" An older man comes into view. He's the man we purchased Conan from, so I gather it's him who owns the house. He looks as though he's never showered.

I stride forward, grab him by the shoulders, and slam him into the wall. "Who was here today?" I'm seething.

His eyes are wide and bounce between me and Bomber. "I… I… don't know." I pull my arm back, ready to punch him. He flinches. "I told you. I don't know," he cries out. "It could have been anyone."

"The group that spends time out back, close to the stores."

He pauses, then his eyes flare, as if recognition sets in. I punch the wall next to his face. "Who. Was. It?" I yell at him.

He jumps before he blurts out, "I think it was Jason and his group of friends."

"How many of them?" I snarl.

His eyes bulge. "Two men… two women. They're young… early twenties."

My body tenses. Fucking four of them!

"Call him… I want them here *now*." My voice threatens violence.

"One of my usuals said the police were here asking questions. Jason won't come back… not now."

My breathing is heavy, my patience wearing thin.

"Where else would they be?" Bomber asks, his voice just as threatening as mine.

"The park… down by the beach."

I slowly let go of him. "If you warn them I'm coming… I'll be back for you!" I let my threat hang in the air.

He abruptly shakes his head. "I won't say anything," he stutters. "I don't get involved."

With that, I turn and leave, get on my bike, pull the throttle back, and race to the park.

I pull into the parking lot and let my bike glide into an empty spot. I get off, hang my helmet over the handlebars, and wait for Bomber. When he gets off his bike and stands beside me, we move as a unit, our eyes searching the tables.

I freeze. "Is that Candy?"

Two guys are sitting down, with what looks like Candy standing and a girl sitting across from the guys. Young-looking. It matches the description.

"It looks like her," Bomber answers.

I growl. "I should have known it was her!" A mix of despair and rage laces my tone.

With every stride, fury pumps adrenaline through my

veins. Bomber is by my side, and when we reach them, they take a second to recognize who we are. They stand to run, but I pull one back and slam him onto the ground. Bomber restrains the other while holding on to the other woman's arm. I hear screams.

Bending over, I grab the guy's shirt. "You beat up my wife?"

Bulging eyes peer back at me, then to my cut. His head whips up to the women. "You stupid sluts! She was from the club?"

I punch him square in the face. One punch... he's out cold. I stand tall and step toward the other man in Bomber's hold. Fear shines brightly in his eyes. "We didn't know," he sputters.

"Like that's going to save you," I say and follow it up by pulling my arm back and punching him in the face. He falls down. There's a dull ache in my hand, but it was well worth it.

Two down... two to go. My death stare zeros in on Candy. She cowers, head bowed, her hands shaking in front of her. "You disgust me," I say, spitting at her feet. Tears fall down her face. "Sophie's not to blame. You have a problem, you take it up with me."

I glower at them, nostrils flaring. "Four against one... you bunch of cowards. If I see any of your faces in this town again, you'll face the fury of the club and Sophie's family." I mean every word.

The other woman frowns and looks at Candy.

I let out a wicked laugh. *They don't know.* "Her name's Sophie *Crown.*"

Blood drains from their faces. *Yeah, that's right... you should be scared.*

Me and Bomber walk back to our bikes. "Can you organize with Rage to check that they've left by tomorrow?"

"Done. Where are you going now?" he asks.

"Back to the hospital. I want to stay by Sophie's side in case she wakes again." Dread envelops me. Sophie's hurt, and the club could face jail time. "If Garrett finds out I'm in any way linked to Sophie's beating, he'll take it out on the club. We're fucked."

I haven't felt like such a burden since my time in foster care, when no one seemed to want me. A burden to Sophie and the club. Everything is my fault. All because I wanted Sophie as my wife. I hang my head in shame. I'm such a selfish asshole. For the first time, I wonder whether it would be better to give her the divorce she wanted in the first place, even though every fiber of my being resists the idea.

When I get to the hospital, I walk down the corridor to Sophie's room. I pull the curtain across and see she's asleep. My heart constricts in pain. It makes me want to return to those men and hit them some more. Lawson and Harrison are sitting on chairs on either side of her. Their gaze shifts upward when I walk in.

"Has she woken up yet?" I ask quietly.

With a frown, Harrison shakes his head.

"I can stay with her if you guys need to go to work," I say to them. "I can message you when she wakes."

Lawson stands, then so does Harrison. "Thanks," Lawson replies. He peers at my knuckles, a small smile lifts his lips. "You might want to clean yourself up." I glance downward and see my swollen hand, dotted with blood.

I dip my head. "I will."

"I hope you put some force behind the punch."

I chuckle. "They were unconscious when I left. I've threatened them to make them leave town. I've got men checking they do just that."

"Them?" Harrison asks. "How many?"

My jaw tightens. "Two men... two women."

Harrison's body stiffens. "You're kidding, right? Four on one…" He shakes his head. "Cowards."

"That's what I said!"

"Well… we'll get out of here. Don't forget to contact us."

"I will," I reply to Lawson. I find the restroom and wash the blood from my hands. When I get back, a nurse is in the room. When her gaze lands on me, her eyes dart away, and she blushes. "How's she doing?" I ask.

"Still the same," the nurse replies.

I lean forward, grab Sophie's hand in mine, and make soothing motions with my thumb. "Do you know how long she'll be in the hospital for?"

"I'm sorry, I don't know. I can find a doctor for you."

"I want Milly when she's free." I trust her… no one else.

The nurse tilts her head. "Do you mean Dr. White?"

Dr. White sounds strange. "Yes, that's her." The nurse gives me a nod and leaves the room.

Hours drift on by. I shift uncomfortably in the seat. The nurse returns a third time. They seem to check on Sophie every hour. The nurse stares at me, then at the ground, and shifts awkwardly on her feet.

"Is there something wrong?" I ask.

"Yes… I mean no… um… you have company… heaps of company. They are in the lobby."

I get up from my seat and walk to see the whole MC sitting in the waiting area. Axle sees me first and moves to me, giving me a manly slap on the back. "I'm sorry, man. We came as soon as we heard."

The women rush over with worry-stricken faces. The other men gather around us. "How is she?" Zara asks with a deep frown on her face. Bomber's arms wrap around her, consoling her.

"Still asleep. The medicine has made her tired."

"Bomber told us what happened," says Reaper.

"I've got flowers," says Elena, who has a bunch of bright yellow and pink flowers in her hand.

"I didn't have time to cook, so I quickly put together some wraps and some snacky food in the bag," Ava says, peering down at the bag in her hands. The men's ol' ladies are amazing women.

"Thank you." My voice echoes my gratitude.

Milly makes her way to us, and everyone quietens and looks at her.

"Do you know how long Sophie will be in the hospital for?" I ask.

"I'll see how she's progressing, but most likely she'll be in here tonight, and from then I just need to ensure that she no longer has any internal bleeding."

"I'll stay with her." I wasn't asking—I had to be here.

"Next time Sophie wakes, we'll move her to a private room. Her father requested all the bells and whistles."

"I'm not surprised." But I'm grateful that she'll have the best care and most comfortable space to make her stay easier.

Milly turns to Reaper. "We can't have all of you see her."

"The women and Viper can go. We'll wait out here," he answers.

The men turn and sit back down in the seats while the women follow me to Sophie's room. After the curtain is pulled back, there's audible gasps.

Droplets trickle down Zara's face as she stands by Sophie's bedside and brushes her hair to the side. "I didn't expect her to look..." I know this can't be easy for Zara, knowing what she's been through.

"Milly, can I have a vase for the flowers?" Elena asks quietly.

Zara puts a black bag on the ground by the bedside table. "I packed her toiletry bag with her toothbrush, hairbrush, makeup, and all the rest of the things she'll need. I packed pajamas and some clothes as well. I knew she wouldn't be happy using the hospital stuff."

The corner of my lip twitches. That's Sophie. "Yes, you're right about that."

"There you go," Milly says, handing Elena a clear vase. Elena puts the flowers in the vase and sets it on the other bedside table.

I press a kiss on the top of Sophie's head, then I take a seat beside her.

"All of you go home. It's okay, I can call if anything changes."

"No." Zara's voice is blunt. "Everyone can go if they need to, Knox and I will be in the waiting room."

"Okay," I reply, knowing I won't persuade Zara. Sophie's like family to her. It's been a pleasure to watch all the women come into their own. How they have all grown and become confident compared to the first time I saw them.

Not long after the women leave, Sophie barely opens one eye. The other still grimly closed from the swelling. "Hey," I say. I stand and lean over to kiss her gently on the lips.

"Hey," she says, her voice still croaky.

"I'm sorry," I say, my tone brittle. "It's my fault."

She puts her hand over mine. "It's not."

I run my other hand through my hair. "I shouldn't have left you, and I should have said something to Candy before she left the clubhouse."

Sophie's eye flares. "How did you know it was her? I didn't tell the police."

Of course she didn't—she protected the club. "When I found the group, Candy was with them. Why didn't you tell the police?"

"They would have told my dad. I didn't want any more tension between you and him. He was already causing enough problems."

I blow out a long, drawn-out breath. "He'll find out. It's only a matter of time."

"I don't blame you. It wasn't your fault." It doesn't minimize the guilt.

A different nurse walks in and smiles at Sophie. "You're awake." Then she looks at me, giving me the once-over. "The other nurses were right… you are handsome."

Sophie lets out a small chuckle, and my chest loosens at seeing the smile on her face.

The nurse goes ahead, performing tests and looking at monitors, and then glances back at Sophie. "How are you feeling?"

"Very tired and a bit tender."

"You're on pain medication, which can make you sleepy."

"Take a seat beside me," Sophie says to me and looks down at the bed.

My eyes roam her bruised face and body and the bandages on her arms. "I can't sit next to you. I don't want to hurt you."

"We're moving you to a private room, which has its own amenities and another bed for a visitor to sleep in," the nurse says. Being rich has its advantages.

"Thank you," Sophie replies.

"I'll have someone wheel you there now." The nurse turns to me. "You go to the waiting area, and I'll come and get you when she's all set up."

"I'll see you soon," I say to Sophie, though it pains me to walk away.

While walking down the corridor, I call Lawson. "Hey, she just woke up."

"Thanks. How is she?"

"Still tired. They're transferring her to the private room now, so I'm just waiting."

"I've spoken to my family, and we'll be there tonight. I'm

just warning you, Dad's still on the warpath, so you may not want to be there when we arrive."

"Does he know who it was?"

"Not yet… why do you ask?"

"Don't worry. I'm not leaving Sophie's side. If your father wants to talk to me, you tell him to do it outside the room. I'm not having it upset Sophie."

He sighs. "I'll try. I'll see you tonight."

Bomber and Zara make their way to me. "We need to have a meeting to discuss everything that's gone down," says Bomber.

I shake my head. "It can wait. I'm not leaving her."

Zara puts a hand on my arm. "I'll stay. You go have your meeting, have a shower, and pack some clothes, and then you can stay here for as long as you want."

There's an ache in the back of my throat. I don't want to leave Sophie.

"I'll be by her side until you arrive. I promise." I can't speak, so I nod at Zara.

I leave with Bomber. When we walk into the clubhouse, everyone's by the bar. Elena and Ava rush to me. "Have there been any changes?" Ava asks.

"Apart from looking like she's been hit by a truck, she's in high spirits."

The women give me a sad smile. "We're here for you," says Ava.

"Church," Bomber shouts.

The men and I make our way into church. I take a seat beside Reaper, who is at the head of the table. I feel the men's stares, the sympathy in their eyes.

"First," Reaper says, "I want to say we are saddened to hear that Sophie was injured."

"Thanks, pres," I reply.

"Do you want to give the club a rundown on what happened?"

"Sure," I reply, as dread rolls my stomach. Being a burden weighs heavy on my shoulders. "Two men and two women attacked Sophie, brutally beating her. I found out one was Candy and the rest were her friends."

"Jealous bitch!" Axle spits.

I peer at Rage. "Did you speak to Bomber?"

He nods. "Yes."

"I gave a warning punch to the men and threatened the women to leave town. I've asked Rage to check that the four of them have left town by tomorrow."

"Does Garrett know it was Candy?" asks Demon.

I flinch. "It's a matter of time. Sophie's family is visiting her tonight. Lawson mentioned that his father is furious. Garrett said if it had anything to do with me, he'll take it out on the club." My gaze flicks from one person to the next. "I'm sorry, I should have divorced Sophie when she wanted it. Then we wouldn't be in shit with her father, and Sophie wouldn't have gotten hurt." Self-loathing consumes me.

"She's your wife," Reaper responds. "You fight for her. It's just unfortunate who her father is."

I snort. "You're telling me."

"We're going to have to come up with a plan for a worst-case scenario. When are you going back to the hospital?" asks Reaper.

"I'm having a shower, grabbing my stuff, then going."

Reaper looks around the table at the men. "I want everyone to think about the best course of action for how to deal with Garrett. We'll reconvene tomorrow when Viper returns."

The clubhouse is quiet, though there's tension in the air. Demon and Cash are by the bar, so I stride to them.

"She'll be feeling better and will be back at the club in no time," says Cash. I appreciate his positivity.

"I hope so," I reply. I stare off, deep in thought. I don't think I'd cope if Sophie got hurt again because of me. I doubt she'll want to be here with me anyway, but on the slight chance she does, I'd love to have a surprise for her, something special for her—if she returns.

TWENTY
TRUTHS UNVEILED

Sophie

I wake to the sound of raised voices.

"That's enough," Viper says. "She's awake." I try to open my eyes, but my left eye resists my efforts. My dad and brothers are standing around me. Viper is at my side, and he gives me one of his loving smiles, though his eyes don't shine as bright.

I peer out the window. It's dark outside, but the fluorescent lights of the hospital are bright. I hear an annoying beep to the side of me. When I lift my hand, I see there's a needle in it, which is attached to a cord and what looks to be an IV bag.

"Hello, sleepy head," Harrison says.

I try to smile back, then clear my throat. "Hey… What time is it?" I ask no one in particular.

"Close to seven-thirty," Alec replies. "Your friend Piper asked that you call her as soon as you can. She wants to fly here to see you."

As much as I want to talk to her, I'm too tired. "I'm

exhausted. Can you tell her I'll call her tomorrow? I'm sure I'll be okay. There's really no need for her to come."

"I'll tell her," Alec answers.

"Can you tell us what you remember?" asks Dad.

My breathing quickens. Viper growls, "She just woke up."

Dad glares at him. He mustn't know of Candy's affiliation with the club yet.

I try to reduce the tension. "Dad, don't be angry. I told the police everything I can remember."

His expression softens ever so slightly. "This would never have happened if you'd stayed at the resort or at home."

Harrison groans beside me. When I peek at him, he subtly rolls his eyes. The last thing I want to do right now is argue.

"It happened outside a liquor store," says Lawson. "It could have happened to her no matter where she was sleeping."

"She wouldn't have been *by herself*," Dad bites back.

I close my eyes and let out a heavy breath.

"When do you get to leave?" asks Harrison.

"Tomorrow or the following day, Milly said."

"You'll be coming home with me, where you can get round-the-clock care during the day," Dad grumbles.

"No, she isn't." Viper raises his voice.

"And you think I'm going to allow you to take care of her?" Dad counters with savage bitterness.

Viper sits up straighter in his chair, his defiant stare aimed at Dad. "I'm capable of looking after her. I'm her husband— she stays with me."

My stomach is doing somersaults at the thought of returning to the clubhouse. When Dad finds out, I don't want to think of what he'll do to the club. But I refuse to stay with Dad. He'll lecture me about Viper and the club.

I rub the side of my head. I sense the movement of the

needle and the cord connected to it. "You're stressing me out," I say loudly.

All eyes land on me. There's a moment of silence before Lawson says, "We'll get going then."

"I'm glad you're okay, sis," says Harrison. Then he cringes. "Even though you look terrible."

I try to swat him, but I'm too slow and he's out of reach. He chuckles as he moves to the door. Alec follows, but Dad stays put.

"Dad," Lawson says, a sliver of warning in his tone.

"I'll be back tomorrow," Dad says.

I look him over. He looks tired. I give him a nod, then he leaves.

Viper waits a moment, his eyes on the door. He walks over, closes it, and then comes back. He bends over, bringing his lips to mine in a quick but loving kiss. His adoring but sad gaze makes my heart flutter.

"Lie down with me?" I ask, needing his body against mine.

"I'll get the bed." He peers off to the side where the visitor's bed is.

"No, I want you here next to me." I shuffle over. At the sharp pain in my ribs, I try my best to keep my face passive.

He frowns, then shakes his head. "No, I don't want to hurt you."

"Please." *I need him.*

His resolve weakens at the desperation in my voice. He gives me a wary stare before he sits. The bed dips under his weight. He lies on his side, and I curl into him. His coconut-and-lime scent sweeps over me. His body against mine soothes me.

"Candy and the people who hurt you are leaving town, so you'll never have to see them again."

Just the mention of her name has me stiffening in his hold.

He gently puts his arm around me and rubs my back. "I'm so sorry." His voice is a whisper, but I can hear the pain in his tone.

I want to tell him it's not his fault, but I'm so tired I'm no longer able to keep my eye open, so I close it and fall back asleep.

A WOMAN GREETS US AS SHE BRINGS MY BREAKFAST TO ME ON A tray. The smell wafts through the room, making my stomach growl. Viper must have moved the other bed beside me. He's giving me a small sleepy smile. His eyes have dark circles under them, like he didn't sleep well.

The woman gives me a polite smile. "I've brought you some scrambled eggs on toast."

"Thank you."

"Where would you like it? I can put it on the bedside table or bring the overbed table around for you."

"Overbed table please." I slowly sit up in bed, flinching at the pain. The nurse rolls the table around and positions it in front of me. She puts the tray down and takes the lid off.

"I've got orange or apple juice, tea or coffee."

"Coffee," I reply.

Viper gets up. "I'll get it for her." Viper and the woman handle my coffee while I eat.

Viper's phone rings. He looks at me, then his phone, then back at me. "It's okay—you can answer it." I bring the coffee to my lips and take a sip. My whole face scrunches up. "Um... can you get a proper coffee?"

Viper nods. "I'll get you one now," he replies.

The woman watches his ass as he saunters away. She turns to me. "He's gorgeous, hon."

"I know," I reply.

After she rolls the food cart out and leaves the room, I look around. My phone is on the bedside table. When I reach over and grab it, I see a long list of missed calls and messages. I bring up Piper's name and call her. She answers on the first ring.

"That was fast," I say through a chuckle.

"I've been waiting for your call. I've been so worried. I wanted to come and see you, but Alec told me you said not to."

"It's a few bumps and bruises. I know you're busy with work."

"Work's not important," she's quick to reply. "My best friend is important."

"I'm okay. There's no need… really."

She sighs. "What happened? Alec said you were attacked but didn't give many details apart from that."

I pause, biting my lip. "Promise you won't say anything to my brother?"

"Yes."

I take a deep breath. "A woman who was in love with Viper, her and her friends saw me waiting outside a store." I swallow the lump in my throat and blink furiously, trying not to cry. "They stole the liquor I had with me and forced me to the ground, where they punched and kicked me."

She gasps, but I keep going. "I've never felt pain like that before. The minutes felt like hours."

"How many were there?" she asks, concern clear in her voice.

"Four."

"No wonder you ended up in the hospital. I hope Viper got them back."

"I think so. They were forced to leave town. I'm glad I won't see them again."

"When are you coming home to New York?" Piper asks sadly.

Viper walks in with a coffee in his hand. His usual swagger has been replaced with tension. His eyebrows are drawn together, and he's staring at me. "Your dad knows." With those words, I feel sick. It's only going to get worse from now on.

"I'll call you later," I tell Piper.

I know my father, and he'll be full of vengefulness. "You need to go!" I tell Viper.

He shakes his head.

"Now!"

He frowns.

"Please…" I plead. "If you love me at all… please let me talk to my father first without you. Go back to the clubhouse, go warn the MC, but I'll try to talk Dad down."

Viper doesn't move. "Please, Viper."

His shoulders fall. He walks over to me, places my coffee on the table, and gives me a hard, lingering kiss. "I'll call you later."

Twenty minutes is all it takes for my father and Alec to arrive.

Dad's face is hard. A vein pulses in his neck. "I knew it!" he roars. "This is why I told you to stay away from the club."

Alec looks out the door and then glances back at Dad. "Calm down."

He glares at Alec. "I will not calm down. Look at your sister," he says, scowling. "She's in the hospital because of him." My breath falters, my heartbeat quickens. The monitor beeps beside me. The numbers keep rising.

Dad and Alec are watching the monitor as well. Dad clears his throat and lowers his voice. "I'm sorry for yelling at you," he says. "But the club is not the right environment for you to stay in. A woman's jealousy landed you in the hospital. Could you imagine if the club develops any enemies? Times that by ten, and that will be the repercussions."

I break eye contact. I hate the doubt Dad puts in my mind. The uncomfortable feeling washes over me again. It could have been a lot worse. I could be dead, and if anything like this happens again… next time I may not be so lucky.

"This is why I always ensured your safety in New York… And talking about New York, what about your business? I'd never seen you so determined, so motivated to do well. You're going to give that all up for a biker that could put you in harm's way?"

Ouch! He digs the knife deeper. Dad's making me think I have to choose between someone I've grown to love being with and my safety and independence. I frown. I shouldn't be made to choose.

He must see the hesitancy on my face because he takes a step closer. "I'll put it this way… if you don't divorce him, I'll ensure the MC gets jail time for the marijuana, and I'm sure they have unregistered firearms and other illegal things on the property. Your relationship with him ends now. I'm not having you risk your safety."

I recoil at the venom in his words. My stomach drops to the floor. I couldn't do that to Viper, the club, or the ol' ladies. And I have no doubt Dad will follow through on his threat. Regardless, I lose Viper. I raise my hand to wipe the corners of my eyes when they start to tear up.

"It's what's best." Dad's voice is softer than before.

There's heat in my cheeks as my blood burns through my body. "Get out!"

Alec's and Dad's eyes widen.

My chest is heaving. "Get out, get out, get out!" Torment is clear in my voice.

They take a step back as the nurse rushes into the room. She looks at me, then my family. "I think it's best you leave."

Dad stiffens. "Do you know how much money I give to this hospital?"

Milly walks in and I release my breath, glad to see her pretty face.

"What is going on here?" she asks, her eyes darting between all of us.

"Sophie asked these two gentlemen to leave. They won't," says the nurse.

Milly pouts and her eyes tighten. "Mr. Crown, we are thankful for your generous donations to the hospital. However…"—she puts her hand on her hip—"Sophie is my patient, and she has asked that you leave. I'd appreciate it if you abide by her wishes." Milly looks at the monitor. "Sophie's heart rate is elevated from stress. She needs rest."

I'm grateful for Milly standing up for me. Few people, let alone a woman, would go toe to toe with my father. I can see the similarities between her and Reaper.

Dad looks back at me. "Okay… we're going… but think about what I've said."

After I watch them go, Milly steps over to me. "Thank you," I tell her, my appreciation apparent.

She smiles. "It's been quite eventful with you here, between Viper, your family, and the MC as well as the nurses having a field day with all the sexy men around. It's been amusing, to say the least."

"How long do I have to stay here for?" I ask while flinching.

"I'd like to perform some tests and a scan to see if your internal bleeding has stopped. At this stage, if it hasn't, I'd like for you to stay another night."

It's going to be much harder if Viper comes back to see me and doesn't leave, wanting me to come back to the clubhouse with him. "Can I leave later this afternoon if it has stopped?"

She studies me. "Yes, you can. Will you have anyone to monitor you?"

I hope I can stay with Lawson. Harrison works shifts and at times stays at the fire station, whereas Lawson might be able to work from home for a day. "Yes," I reply, but I don't mention who. I don't think Milly would say anything, but I don't want to risk her telling the club I'm leaving to stay with my brother.

Sophie

"Here, let me get that for you," says Lawson, passing me the TV remote.

"I can get it," I snap. I give him a tight smile. I don't enjoy being dependent on anyone, but here I am, feeling useless. Lawson raises his hands in surrender.

As I lean over to retrieve the remote, a twinge of pain shoots through my ribs. There's a chuckle across from me.

"If I knew you were going to be a bitch to look after, I would have left you in the hospital."

"Sorry," I mutter under my breath. "I hate feeling like this." My body aches all over, especially my ribs, but it's the ache in my chest that hurts the most.

"At least you'll be healed by Zara and Knox's photos at the wedding."

My sharp intake of breath makes me cough. I forgot about Zara and Bomber's wedding. I have to go—I wouldn't miss it for the world—but it's going to be hard to fake being okay when I see Viper and the whole MC again.

My phone rings, but I don't answer it because I know it'll be Viper and I don't have it in me to talk to him… not tonight. The ringing stops, but moments later it chimes, which suggests I have a voicemail. Followed by Lawson's phone ringing.

He raises a brow at me, grabs his phone, answers it, and puts it on loudspeaker.

"Where is she?" Viper asks. I frown at the worry in his voice.

"Sophie's safe. She's staying with me."

There's a heavy breath through the phone. "Why did she leave? She didn't tell me, and she won't answer her phone."

"Whatever is going on is between you two, I'm not getting involved. Sophie's still in pain, she's tired, and…"—Lawson looks me dead in the eyes and says—"she's being a bitch. I think I'm doing you a favor. Anyway, she's here, she's fine. Just give her a bit of space and I'm sure she'll contact you soon."

"She's my wife."

My head falls back from the sadness in his voice. There's a painful tightness in my chest. I'm delaying the inevitable. I don't know how I'm going to tell him. I know if I tell him the truth, he won't accept it. It pains me to have to hurt him, but I can't be the reason the MC ends up in jail either.

"As I said, try calling her again tomorrow."

"If she doesn't pick up tomorrow, I'll be at your doorstep."

Lawson sighs. "Okay, Viper. I'll let her know."

After they hang up, Lawson shakes his head while his eyes are on me. "What are your plans with him?"

"Dad gave me an ultimatum. Divorce and leave Viper or he'll ensure one way or another that the whole MC ends up in jail."

Lawson's mouth parts. "I can have a word with Dad if you want."

"There's no point. He won't listen."

"I feel bad for you. He's always been tougher on you than the rest of us."

And don't I know it. "When's enough, enough? At this rate, he's going to turn me into one of those single crazy cat ladies."

Lawson chuckles. "He wants you to be with someone he approves of." His face pinches. "Not that anyone will meet his expectations."

"I understand Dad didn't approve of me getting married to a biker and he wants me safe. He even mentioned me losing my drive for my business in New York, as if I'm giving it all up to stay married."

"I'm sure he made a compelling argument. It's a shame he has so much influence over the MC because I've seen how happy you've been since you've been back."

I swallow over the lump in my throat.

"You understand that if you don't talk to Viper, he'll come here."

I wrap my arms around myself and squeeze. "I know… I'll talk to him tomorrow." I struggle to keep the emotion out of my voice.

"And what are you going to say?"

"I don't know yet," I admit sadly.

I go into the spare bedroom and lie down, trying to ignore my aching body. I pull the duvet over me, snuggle into the pillow, and sniffle as the tears stream down my face.

Feeling warmth, I open my eyes to the sun filtering in through the curtains. There's a dull throb in my head from last night. My eyes are still raw from crying.

After a shower and a coffee, my phone rings again, making my heart beat faster. I stare at the phone vibrating next to me before answering. "Hello."

"Sophie." Viper's exasperated. "Why have you been ignoring my calls? I'll come and get you… I want to take care of you."

I briefly close my eyes and pause. "I'm sorry." My voice breaks. "I can't do this charade anymore. I want a divorce."

"What charade?" he bites back. "That's not the deal."

"Our marriage was a mistake. I was there for a good time." I cringe at my lie. "That time is over, and I'm going back to New York."

"You're lying!"

He knows me all too well. I gaze up at the ceiling and blink, trying not to cry. "It's done. Bye, Viper." My heart shatters, and I can't stop the tears from falling hard and fast. I cry until I'm empty.

Eventually, I gather the strength to get up and wash my face. I take my pain medication, put on another comfortable pair of pajamas, lie on the lounge, and sulk. This is why I never got attached to men. In the end, I'm left alone with a gaping hole in my heart. A hole where Viper used to be.

Our relationship began because of drinking and progressed due to blackmail. And then I got attacked by Viper's ex. I should have known it was inevitable that our relationship would end… even though I didn't want it to because I fell hard for him. Even under the circumstances, I didn't want to think about the future because I was too happy in the present. I should have taken Dad more seriously. The warning, the interference with the fight, the threats. He knew I wouldn't allow the MC to go to jail.

There are three loud knocks on the door, and it makes me jump. "Open up, Sophie," Viper's voice filters through.

My breath hitches. I'm paralyzed until he knocks again.

"I know you're in there. I'm not going anywhere until I talk to you."

I force myself up and walk to the front door. Each step fills me with fear. I slowly unlock it, willing myself to calm down and taking a second to compose myself. I leave the latch lock connected so that the door will open only an inch or two.

His eyes capture mine, holding me prisoner in their depths. There's a deep frown on his gorgeous face. I take deep breaths and force my hands to stay where they are, to keep myself from unlocking the door and walking into his arms.

"Why are you doing this?" His voice is soft and sincere.

I open my mouth to answer, but I end up closing it again.

"Is it because of Candy? She's left town, I checked."

I shake my head.

"It's your father, isn't it? What did he say to you? You were fine until you spoke to him."

I knew I couldn't hide it from Viper, but I try to keep my face passive and shove those emotions down deep… even for a few minutes. He can't approach Dad. It will make everything worse. "No… I have a life in New York. My business, my friends. It's all there. I moved away from Crown Village to make something of myself. I won't give that up." My voice is steady, though the heartache on Viper's face crushes my soul. My hand flies to my mouth. "I'm sorry," I mutter, then close the door.

I slide down as another sob rips from my chest. I struggle to draw air into my lungs. Lawson rushes out of his room and to me. My vision is blurry as he bends down and picks me up off the floor, bringing me over to the lounge again, where he places me down ever so gently.

Soon after, there's a duvet over me. A memory flashes. Alec used to do this when we were kids, playing the big brother role. Even though we don't see eye to eye, I should give him more of a break. It was the nannies who looked after us, but he tried to do his best, even though he wasn't much older than us.

I roll over and close my eyes, hoping sleep can take away some of the pain. I wish it could be different between me and Viper, but it isn't.

In the afternoon, a knock on the door wakes me up. My heart pumps harder as I patiently wait for Lawson to see who it is. I hear muffled voices and then Zara, Ava, and Elena come into view. As I sit up to greet them, I look down at my attire. I'm sure I look like a mess.

Zara rushes to me and gives me a tight hug. I flinch from the pain. "Sorry," she says, then sits beside me. "How are you doing?"

Ava and Elena give me sad smiles and also sit down. "Okay, I guess… Thanks for coming to see me." I try to sound cheery but fail.

Zara puts her hand over mine. "You don't have to be strong all the time."

I press my lips into a hard line, trying not to cry. "How's Viper?" The tormented look he gave me before he left… I'll never forget it.

"He's hurting," says Elena. "Him and Axle are close, and even Axle's worried about him. They were having a few drinks as we were leaving."

I look at the three of them in turn. "I never intended to hurt Viper."

"We know that," Ava replies.

"What did he tell everyone?" I ask curiously. I'm sure everyone hates me for hurting him.

"All he said was that you're going back to New York and

that you've asked for a divorce," says Zara. She studies me. "Was there something else?"

I take a moment to gather my composure. "I have responsibilities in New York. I have my business and my best friend. I've enjoyed staying here in Crown Village, but the attack…" I peer at the floor and then back up. "It scared me. My father is intolerable as well. I've loved spending time with you, the MC, and my brothers, but being here was short-term." Even though I try, I can't stop the tears from falling.

"I'm sorry, Sophie," says Zara. "I thought you two were really great together."

We were.

TWENTY-TWO
DESPAIR

Viper

A WEEK PASSES. I'M SITTING ON THE EDGE OF THE BED, TWIRLING the wedding ring around my finger, wondering why Sophie changed her mind within a day of me seeing her. She held on to me in the hospital like she didn't want me to leave her side. I saw the sadness in her eyes when I went to see her at Lawson's. All I wanted to do was break the door down and hold her when she was crying. It makes me think it was her father forcing her hand.

I've been to Lawson's apartment a few times after Sophie ended it, but he wouldn't let me see her. I thought that if I told Sophie I love her, it could be enough for her to stay. I want her to hear me out before leaving, but at the same time, I want nothing to happen to the club. The club's my life, and the people in it are my family.

My jaw tightens at what happened. If I had more time to prove to Garrett that I can care for his daughter, that I love her, I'd like to think he would at least give me a chance to show him, but Candy ruined that for me. I thought Candy was a cool chick, but I never had feelings for her like I do for Sophie. I never thought she would go to the lengths of physically harming Sophie.

Garrett was right: I shouldn't have left Sophie by herself. Within our town, I thought she'd be safe, but instead she got hurt because of me. The world weighs heavily on my shoulders. Being in an MC comes at a cost and can be dangerous for ol' ladies. I don't think I could live with myself if something happened to her again because of me.

I let out a heavy breath and run a hand through my hair for what feels like the hundredth time today. My thoughts are radical, going from one extreme to the other. It's been hard thinking Sophie would be better off without me. I know she has strong feelings for me, but she's independent, and her business means a lot to her. It shouldn't be black and white. She was managing her business fine from Crown Village.

I'm sure it's hard for her to be away from her friends, but she has her family here. She's close to her brothers, and she has Zara. She also seemed to get along well with the other ol' ladies.

There's a knock on my door.

"Come in."

Reaper walks in. He leans against the wall as his eyes survey my face. "How are you doing?"

"Pretty shitty."

"I'm here if you want someone to talk to."

I glance away, trying to think of how to explain my jumbled thoughts. "Look at what happened to her because of me. The club's better off without her because of the trouble her father has caused… but I don't want to let her go, and it's tearing me up, and I don't know what to do."

He bobs his head. "I can't tell you what to do, but I can say… she's not better off without you. From what I saw, you were both genuinely happy. Trust me… when you find that person, you don't let them go. You fight for your relationship. I believe you and Sophie could find a way to make Garrett listen. She's his daughter, he's overprotective, but I find it hard to believe he would want to see her upset and miserable."

There's a brief silence. "It took a while for Ava to feel safe again, after what happened, but I was there for her every step of the way."

"But… what about the club? I don't want to cause more damage than I already have. What would you choose? The club or Ava?"

"I'd make it work for everyone… whatever it takes."

I nod. "Thanks for the talk, pres."

"Any time," he answers.

He's right. I grab my phone and pull up Harrison's name.

"Hey," he answers. "I'm sorry to hear about you and Sophie."

"About that… do you know if Sophie has left yet?"

"She left yesterday."

Already. "Did she end up mentioning why she had the sudden change of heart to go back to New York?"

"Didn't she tell you?"

"No, she didn't." Not the real reason.

"I'm loyal to my sister, but you're the first guy I've seen her fall for and care about. I think you ground her and you're decent, so… it was all Dad."

"I knew it!"

"Lawson said he would ensure that the whole MC ended up in jail."

I huff, though Garrett could if he wanted to, knowing his

reach and how much power he holds within this town. Sophie protected me… protected the club.

"Would there be any way to change your father's mind about me and the club? What do I have to do? We aren't terrible people—we help a charity for women and children. The townspeople might be wary of us, but they know if they need help, we're there for them. Candy's no threat anymore. I made her leave town, and we don't have enemies." I rub my forehead. "I don't know what else to do."

He lets out a heavy sigh. "I don't think there is anything you can do. It rests with Sophie. Only she can change his mind. She isn't talking to him at the moment, and his mood swings are worse than normal, so I'd say it's affecting him."

The edge of my lip twitches. "Good! He deserves it." I pause as a thought comes to mind. "Is she going to the wedding?"

"We all are."

The thought of seeing her again ignites a rush of emotions. I crave more moments by her side. It was nowhere near enough. "I look forward to seeing all of you there."

After I hang up, I glance at my bed. It's not the same without her. Loneliness engulfs me. There's a void inside me because she took a part of me when she left.

I want to prove to her that she's been on my mind. I put my phone in my pocket and go downstairs to see Demon, Axle, and Rage sitting at the bar. I look between the three of them. "Just the three men I wanted to see." Especially Demon, because he's good at building things. "Are you guys free this afternoon?"

Axle nods. "Free as a bird."

"Can you come to the hardware store with me?"

Demon raises a brow, the corner of his mouth tilts up. "What are we building?"

"A gym."

"Yessss," Rage cheers. "I'm happy with that. It would be good to have a setup of everything here." He pauses. "You should organize a church meeting. I'm sure everyone will want to contribute."

I nod. "Good idea. Let's do it."

TWENTY-THREE
BLAME GAME

Sophie

"Sophie… Sophie…"

I look at Maddy, the manager of my business. "Sorry, what did you say?"

She smiles. "Your flowers have arrived." Joy fills my broken heart. I peer at the flowers on my desk, which are perishing. Viper has sent me flowers every Monday of every week, going on four weeks now.

"Would you like me to replace the ones on your desk again?"

"Yes, please."

She takes the vase and comes back from the kitchen with the new bunch of long-stemmed red roses. They are beautiful. I should tell him to stop sending them, but I can't bring myself to do it. They're the only thing that improves my mood, and it's nice to know he's still thinking of me.

"Have you approved that invoice to replenish the stock?"

I sigh. I forgot. I can't think straight. Slapping a smile on my face, I say, "I'll do it now."

Maddy has been doing an incredible job managing the business while I've been away. I've been trying to bury myself in work, but she's been on top of everything, making that task impossible. It's been great to take a step back and rely on the employees. It's less stressful, and it's shown me I don't have to micromanage or be at the business every day to make it run smoothly. Which is annoying, because it means I could have managed it from Crown Village… I *could* be with Viper.

He has consumed my mind every minute of every day, and I'm starved of his presence. It hasn't been long, but I miss him, and the thought of not being able to get over him horrifies me. It was much simpler when I slept with men with no strings attached.

I know I won't be able to find that passion and connection with someone else. Not that I want to. He's weaved himself into the core of my existence. He'll always be a part of me.

My teeth clench together. All because of my father and his persistent need to control my life.

My office phone rings.

"Hello."

"Hi, it's your father again," says Maddy. "Would you like to talk to him?"

I flinch. "No, tell him I'm out of the office."

"Uh… okay."

I have sympathy for Maddy, being on the other end of my father's phone calls. I can imagine he's taking his frustration out on her, but I refuse to talk to him when he's holding my happiness hostage.

There's this pull to go back to Crown Village, but I can't. I can't be the reason the MC men end up in jail, but I'm struggling. I put up a strong front, but I feel brittle. My stomach churns. It doesn't feel right without him.

My phone beeps. When I glance down, I see a message from Zara. She's been messaging me every couple of days since I left. She asks how I'm doing, and I always ask her how Viper is doing. She said he's quieter than normal, but he's been busy with a project. I'm curious about what's taking up his time, but when I ask Zara, she always says she can't tell me.

I close her message, then see Viper's name underneath with a blue dot next to it that shows there are unread messages. My finger hovers over his name, but I stop myself. I had thoughts of changing my number or blocking his, but I can't. I pick up my bag off the floor, stand, and hang it over my shoulder. I'm driving myself crazy. I need to get out of here.

I go home, get changed, and go to the gym. After I put my belongings away in a locker, I make my way over to the treadmills. I choose a treadmill that has no one next to it and hop on. I set a pace and incline and start off in a steady stride as the next song plays in my earbuds: "Love Game" by Lady Gaga. As I listen to the lyrics, I inwardly groan at the thought of Viper. I'm here to forget him.

I skip to the next track and up the pace of the treadmill until I'm jogging. I crave the exhaustion… the mental relief. "Night and Day" by Silver Sneakers comes on, which yet again reminds me of our relationship. "You've got to be kidding me," I mumble to myself.

My breathing becomes heavier as my heart beats faster, and it's not just the jogging causing it. I push through, keeping up a consistent pace as sweat mists my skin. "I Want You to Know" by Zedd and Selena Gomez is next, and I can't deal. I pull my earbuds out and slam them down on the stand by my water bottle.

I turn the pace up again until I'm running. I focus on my stride, running in sync with the treadmill. My lungs burn, and I'm dripping with sweat. I push myself further and keep going until I can't anymore. I turn the pace down while heaving, trying to draw in air.

When the pace turns into a slow walk, I grab the towel and wipe my face. I sense a presence beside me. It's a man. He's smiling at me. He's tall, with bulging muscles. I don't recognize him. "Can I help you?" I ask while pressing the Stop button.

"You did well." His eyes drag the length of me slowly. "You're fit. I know I'm being forward here, but I wanted to see if I could take you out sometime."

I stare at him. Is he serious? He's hitting on me while I'm sure I look like a drowned rat. My eyes drift over him. His arms are crossed, and his arms and traps are bulging. If I'd never met Viper, I'd most likely take him up on his offer. I could use a distraction, but I feel ill at the thought of another man's hands on me. A twinge of pain spikes my chest.

I lift my hand, giving him a tight smile. "I'm married." Though I don't know for how long.

He chuckles. "That means nothing to me."

Yuck! I hate sly people like that. "No, thanks," I reply curtly, grab my things, and leave.

Once I get home, I walk inside, put my bag by the kitchen counter, and take a seat.

Piper walks out and gives me a small smile. She points. "There's mail for you."

I grab the envelope, open it, and pull out the piece of paper.

Dear Sophie,

I understand why you're doing this.

Please know that I love you and I'll always be waiting for you.

Love always,
Brayden
P.S. I'm not signing any divorce papers until you bring your sexy ass back to Crown Village.

I chuckle as tears fall on the piece of paper, blurring the ink.

Piper's arms come around me. "I've never seen you so upset before. You love Viper, I can tell."

"I do," I reply and sniffle. It doesn't matter what I do or where I go. The memories of Viper are engraved inside my mind.

My phone rings in my bag. Piper lets go of me and grabs my bag off the floor, placing it in front of me. I unzip it to see my father's name flash on the screen. My teeth grind as burning anger pushes through the sadness.

I answer it. "Stop calling me!"

"Sophie, you can't keep ignoring me forever. It's very childish."

"You can't force me to talk to you. After what you've done to me, our relationship is rocky at best."

"You weren't with him for long, so I don't know why you're blowing it out of proportion."

My eyes open wide. "I love him, Dad, and you ruined that for me."

He's quiet.

"Don't call me again. I mean it… Unless you're going to fix the damage you've caused, I don't want to hear what you've got to say."

"You can't be serious!"

"Try me… I am your daughter. I've learned from the best in how to get my own way. Bye, Dad!" Anger sears me. It's never-ending with him when it comes to Viper. I was always so concerned with not making waves between me and him. He's the only parent I have left, but this wasn't my fault. He's gone too far this time, and I'm going to make sure he knows it.

Piper claps from beside me. "I've never heard you talk to your dad like that before."

"I usually don't, but he's crossed a line. For so long, all I wanted was his approval and for him to be proud of what I've accomplished. No matter how hard I tried, I never felt I achieved that."

She frowns. "He's your dad. I think even as adults we crave approval from our parents."

"After all that, when I was finally at the point where my business was running well without me having to be there all the time, I was at home spending time with my brothers, and I finally found a genuine relationship.

"My relationship with Viper might have started off fake, but it grew to be so much more than that. He saw the real me. He showed me again and again that I was it for him, and Dad ruined that. Ending up in the hospital scared me, but Viper was by my side. Dad destroyed my chance to be happy and give my relationship with Viper a proper go, and I hate him for that. And to be honest, I don't know if I'll be able to forgive him." I said the truth out loud. Dad's not only ruining my relationship with Viper, but also with him.

"I understand," Piper replies. "If I was in your shoes, I'd feel the same way. As selfish as it sounds, I'd hate for you to leave"—she frowns—"but I want you to be happy. So, if you and Viper work out, I understand if you leave to go back home. Even though I'll miss you, please know I want what's best for you."

My eyes blur with fresh tears. "Thank you," I reply, a little choked up from her kind words. I jump up and hug her tightly. It's the acceptance I desperately need from my father.

"When's the wedding?"

My heart beats faster just at the thought of having to see everyone again, especially Viper. "In one month."

"That's coming up quickly… Are you still going?"

I nod. "Bomber and Zara mean a lot to me. That day is a special day for them. It's not about me, so as hard as it's going to be, I want to be there to celebrate with them. They have been through hell together but have come out the other end stronger than ever."

TWENTY-FOUR
WEDDING

Viper

I spray the cologne on me that I know Sophie loves and go downstairs to meet the rest of the men. Bomber is by the front door, leaning against the wall, fidgeting. It makes me smile. He's always self-assured and in control, so to see him so anxious is highly amusing.

I walk up to him and slap his back. "You're not going to throw up, are you?"

He shakes his head, though he doesn't look one-hundred-percent sure, which makes me laugh. "You've got nothing to be anxious about. Remind me to thank Zara for allowing us to wear our cuts and jeans. I'm so glad she didn't make us dress up in those clown suits and ties."

Zara's friendly and down to earth. Everyone's ol' ladies are. There's no bullshit drama with them, and we all get along. Sophie fit in so well with them and the other men. She belongs here with us.

"If it's okay with you, I was hoping to talk to Garrett

tonight at the wedding reception, though I don't have to if you don't want me to." I'd understand if Bomber doesn't want me to have a serious conversation with Garrett at their wedding. I shouldn't be selfish, but I don't know if I'll get a chance again to talk to Garrett and Sophie face to face on the same night.

"Go ahead, but if it gets heated, I'd prefer for you two to organize the discussion for another day."

That's fair.

Axle walks over. "I can't believe you're getting married," he says to Bomber. "You're the second, after me of course... though Reaper and Ava are practically married..." His eyes skim all the men as we wait for Reaper. "But you're most likely the last of us to get married too."

I clear my voice. "I was the second."

"Oh yeah... I forgot about you. You were the second to get married and the first to get divorced."

Low blow. I barge his shoulder.

Axle smirks. "Too soon?"

"Dick," I mumble under my breath, knowing he's only playing. "I haven't signed any papers."

"Sophie was funny. I liked her," Axle replies. "Is she coming tonight?" Axle asks.

"All of my family will be there," replies Bomber. "Except my mom, for obvious reasons."

Axle glances at me. "It's shit that protecting the club has to come at the cost of your relationship. I know how much you like her. You must be stoked you're seeing her tonight though."

A rush of endorphins surges through me. My lip curves up as I smile. "I can't wait to see her."

Reaper moves toward us with knitted brows.

"What's up, pres?" I ask him.

"Ava's been up vomiting all night again."

"You don't have to come to the wedding," says Bomber.

He gives us a funny look. "There's no way she would stay and miss out. She doesn't care if she takes something with her to vomit into."

"She's really popped out," Axle chimes in.

"Yep," Reaper says proudly. "About four weeks to go."

Reaper peers at Bomber. "Are you excited for your wedding?"

"He's nervous," I reply for him.

Bomber narrows his eyes at me. He'd never admit it.

As we walk out of the clubhouse, I feel the best I've felt in months at the thought of celebrating Bomber and Zara's wedding… And maybe I can save my marriage too.

AFTER WE PULL INTO THE PARKING LOT, WE WALK THROUGH THE amusement park and to the hall where the ceremony and reception will be held. Having the wedding at the amusement park holds sentimental value for Zara.

With every step, my heart beats a little faster at the thought of seeing Sophie. As we walk inside, there's a hum of conversation, with people sitting in rows on either side of an aisle.

The hall is decked with roses and fancy white decorations. From what I heard, the women and Zara's parents have been working on it for the last two days. It looks great. Bomber and Twitch move to the front podium, toward Zara's parents and the priest.

The wide-eyed look on the priest's face has me chuckling. I bet he wishes he wasn't the one doing this wedding. I scan the room for Sophie and see the back of her brothers' and father's heads on the left-hand side of the room toward the front. I make my way over until I'm standing by them.

Harrison and Lawson stand, give me a smile, and shake my hand. "Hey, man. Good to see you," I say to Harrison.

"You too," he replies.

Alec stands next. He shakes my hand but doesn't smile, though I'm used to his cold behavior.

Garrett gives me the slightest head tilt in acknowledgment. My eyes open wide. He's the one who caused me to lose the only woman I've ever had feelings for. A part of me despises him, but I know I've got to bury that, especially if I want to have a word with him later on.

I lean in close to Lawson and lower my voice. "Where's Sophie?"

"She's with the other women at the front," Lawson replies.

Nerves make my stomach coil. More people are coming in and taking their seats. "Well… I better get going. I presume I sit on the other side," I say with a head tilt to the right.

"That's correct," says Alec.

I glance down at my jeans, shirt, and MC cut. They are in suits. I wonder if me being a biker influenced Sophie's decision to leave. Maybe she had no intention of staying with me. I shake my head at the toxic thoughts.

As I walk by Bomber's family, I smile and greet them, then slide into the seat next to Axle just as the music starts to play. Bomber is standing at the podium in front of the priest. As I scan the crowd, Sophie, Elena, and Ava take their seats in the front row.

Sophie has her hair all done up. It's something simple that shows off her shoulders and neck, which is sexy as hell.

Everyone turns toward the back of the hall, where Zara is slowly walking step by step, her arm linked through her father's. She looks beautiful and has gone with a black wedding dress instead of a white one. It suits them as a couple, as Bomber isn't dressed in a traditional suit either.

Zara smiles at the crowd of people, making everyone smile back at her. When they reach the podium, her father hands her off to Bomber, and they smile at each other. I'm happy for them, but I can't deny the twinge of jealousy at Zara and Bomber being able to spend the rest of their lives with each other.

I stare at Sophie again. Our eyes lock. It's physically painful to see her. She gives me a sad smile, then glances back at the bride and groom. The sooner I talk to Garrett, the better.

Sophie

During and after the wedding photos, I've kept myself busy by helping with everything I can to distract me from Viper. Anything to keep my distance, because this whole wedding has stirred up a mix of emotions within me. Anger, resentfulness, and sadness threaten to drown me.

I spot a waiter carrying a tray of champagne flutes, and I bolt straight toward him and grab two glasses. I down the first, take a deep breath, relax my shoulders, and begin to sip the next one like a lady.

Hands on my shoulders make me squeak and jolt, nearly splashing my drink everywhere. Luckily, I have a firm grip on it. It's Harrison with one of his easy smiles on his face.

"How are you doing? You look stressed."

"I am."

"Have you spoken to Dad yet?"

I huff. "I keep walking away from him. I've done my best to avoid him."

He gives me a sad smile. "I can tell he misses you."

I dab the corners of my eyes. "Well, being without Viper is destroying me."

He pulls me into a hug.

"Everyone, take your seats," says Reaper over the microphone. "Everyone, welcome the newlyweds," he says as Bomber and Zara walk in, holding hands and smiling. Everyone claps, and there's a mix of cheers, hollers, and wolf whistles from the MC men. Zara and Knox take a seat at the table at the head of the room.

As I make eye contact with Viper, I'm struck with sorrow at the sad smile on his face. *He feels it too.* The hollow ache of knowing I'm missing out on a future with Viper.

I can't concentrate on the toasts by Zara's and Bomber's parents. Instead, I glance down at my wedding ring. I've been meaning to take it off, but I can't. *I don't want to get divorced.*

I emerge from my dreamlike state when people start clapping.

"Now for the father and daughter dance," says Reaper. Zara's father meets her at her table and takes her hand as they walk to the middle of the dance floor. He twirls her around first as they smile at each other. The music plays, and they waltz together. I dab at the corners of my eyes and blink rapidly, trying not to allow the tears to fall. I wish I had that kind of relationship with my father.

"Excuse me," I mutter under my breath. I put the napkin on the table, gently pull my chair out, and rush down the corridor toward the restroom.

"Sophie!" I hear my name being called. I turn to see my father, and behind him is Viper. Worry is etched on their faces.

I glare at my father. "You don't get to comfort me. You stopped me from having my first healthy relationship with him." I gesture over Dad's shoulder. He turns and looks at Viper before looking back at me.

"I'm trying to keep you safe."

"No," I hiss. "You're trying to control me. You think you know what's best for me, but you don't."

Viper steps forward. Dad's mouth opens, but he glances at Viper, then back to me.

"Do you want to know why I'm so worried about your safety?" Dad asks. There's a sadness in his voice that I've never heard before.

I inch back from him, surprised there's a reason beyond his arrogant overprotectiveness. "Yes, I do."

"Your mother is why."

I suck in a sharp breath. "What about Mom?" He never talks about her.

"She was kidnapped when she was pregnant with Harrison due to a business deal going south."

My heart crashes against my ribcage. "Is that why she left?" I ask. It comes out as a whisper.

"No. I don't think she ever planned to stay. She admitted that she wasn't cut out for motherhood, and being kidnapped further reinforced her belief that she didn't want a family. As a result, she willingly signed over all parental rights to me."

"And she never came home to see us?" My voice hitches at the end.

He lets out a heavy breath. "I begged her to stay, but we grew apart, and she said she never felt the bond between herself and you and your brothers. I think she thought she was doing what was right, and nothing I said could have made her stay."

Everything falls into place. "Where is she now?"

"She travels for work, so she could be anywhere right now."

I nod and rub the base of my throat. I step into my father's arms, the anger washed away by the heartache in his voice. I understand his incessant need to keep me safe. When Dad pulls away, I see his eyes glisten. I desperately need Viper right now, so I clear my throat. "I need to sit down with you and with my brothers and discuss it, but right now is not the time. Can we talk about it later?"

He nods and slowly walks away from us.

I step into Viper's outstretched arms. He holds me, supporting me like he always does.

"I'm so sorry," he says in a soothing voice as he rubs my back. His scent, his warmth are what dims the pain.

I pull back, my face flushed. "I'm going to have to check my makeup." I don't want anyone to see I'm upset and put a damper on the night.

"I'll wait." He glances at the floor briefly. "I'll always wait for you."

I give him a sad smile and try to blink away my glassy eyes. I go to the restroom to fix my makeup, and when I come out, Viper is leaning against the wall, waiting for me. He's glancing down at his phone with a smile on his face.

"What are you looking at?"

He turns his phone around. It's a photo of us on our wedding night. It looks as though we're both laughing while staring into each other's eyes, and it hits home. I'm making Dad change his mind, but after our emotional discussion, I can't bring myself to ask, not tonight.

Viper puts his phone in his pocket and cups my face, making me look up at him. He brings his lips to mine in a soft but loving kiss that he holds a little longer.

"I've missed you. My life isn't the same without you. We belong together," he breathes against my mouth.

I gaze into his adoring eyes. "I love you."

He leans back down, giving me another kiss. "I love you too."

His hands fall from my face and he grabs my hand. "Can I have this dance?" he asks, all charming and sexy as hell.

I smile back and squeeze his hand. "Yes, you can." I follow him out and to the dance floor, where the band is playing and everyone's out of their seats dancing. Viper leads me through the crowd and toward the middle of the dance floor, where Elena and Zara are dancing together. Axle is next to them, sporting some very goofy dance moves, doing a mix of the lawnmower and the sprinkler. It makes me chuckle.

Viper pulls my body flush against his. My heart feels full being in his arms, where our problems drift away as we smile at each other, where nothing else matters but us.

After the cake cutting and once the night comes to an end, dread creeps in. As the last guests leave and only my, Zara's, and Bomber's families and the MC are left, we help return the hall back to the way it was.

"Are you coming to the party at the MC?" asks Viper as we put away the last chairs.

I smile and put out my hand. He interlocks his fingers with mine, and we leave together.

JUDGEMENT

Viper

Sophie rides to the clubhouse on the back of my motorcycle. I love her squeals of joy as I accelerate down the road and she hugs me tighter. I take a deep breath, soaking in the ride.

When we arrive, I peer back at Sophie as she gets off the bike. Our time is limited. I want to delve in and capture her soul, to keep hers with mine. I just want her to stay with me. I might have claimed her as my wife, but she fucking owns me, and I know no one else can take her place.

She hasn't asked me to sign the divorce papers, so that's the small hope I'm hanging on to, and there's no way I'm bringing it up.

"Come with me. I have a surprise for you," I say to her.

Sophie stills. "A surprise?" she asks. "What is it?"

"You'll just have to wait and see."

There's a pinch in her face. "If I recall correctly, the last surprise was a month-long blackmail pact."

I give her a smile. "But it was worth it, wasn't it?"

She smiles back. "Yes, it was."

We walk through the clubhouse. My body tingles with anxiety. When we reach the back door, I turn the back light on and then slip in behind Sophie and cover her eyes with my hand. "Close your eyes."

"Okay," she answers.

I open the door. "There are two steps," I remind her. She laughs as we leisurely move forward. When our feet meet the ground, I encourage her to move forward until we reach the undercover area. My heart beats faster, as I take my hands away. "Open them."

She stops momentarily, then gasps. Her hand flies to her mouth. I watch her as she gawks at all the new gym equipment. She steps forward, touching the treadmill rail. Then she goes to the weights and walks to the cable machine. She clears her throat before she glances up at me, though her eyes are glassy. "You did this," she says as she looks around, "for me?"

"I wanted you to have something here that you love. Don't get me wrong, me and Rage and some of the men wanted it too, but I did it for you."

She rushes to me. Her petite body collides with mine and she throws her arms around my neck as I encircle her waist. I lift her feet off the ground and twirl her around in my arms.

When her feet meet the ground again, she says, "Thank you… it means a lot that you thought about me."

"I'm always thinking of you." A couple of tears fall down her face. I wipe them from her cheeks.

"I'd better get going. You stay… I'll call the limousine to pick me up."

I take her hand in mine. "I'll take you." Every minute with her is a blessing.

She shakes her head and pulls her hand away. "I'm

staying in Crown Village for a couple of days, so I'll talk to you soon," she says in a small voice.

Misery swirls through me. I want to rush to her, convince her to stay here, but I can't do that this time.

I go upstairs and force myself to go straight to bed. I'm not up for celebrations. Tonight gave me an insight into why Sophie's dad is so hellbent on keeping her safe. He doesn't want to lose someone else, but he's forcing me and Sophie to endure the same fate as him—losing the person we love. How can't he see that?

I exhale loudly and roll onto my side. It's not fucking fair! I seem to always be the one who loses people. My own parents didn't want me. I craved a family, so I joined the military. I've lost brothers in war but found a group of men I've built solid relationships with.

This club is everything to me, and when I finally found an amazing woman to have as my ol' lady, she's forced to leave me. I don't understand why I always miss out on being loved… Why can't I have what other people have… why is it always out of reach?

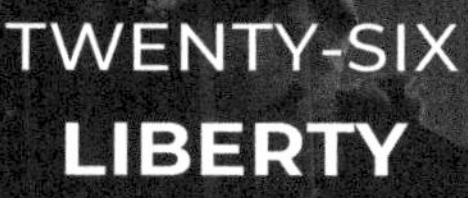

TWENTY-SIX
LIBERTY

Sophie

THE PAIN ON VIPER'S FACE REPLAYS IN MY HEAD LIKE A nightmare. I can still hear his tortured voice, his pain reflecting my own. I know I can't keep living like this. It's my life, and I refuse to let my father have control over it anymore. The limousine pulls up outside the home I grew up in.

My chest tightens. I hated seeing the pain on Dad's face. I appreciate his honesty, but his past shouldn't dictate my future. I walk through the house, and when I see Dad sitting on the lounge with his laptop on his lap, I struggle to catch my breath. He glances up and studies me. Then he slowly closes his laptop and places it beside him.

I clear my throat. "Do you love me?"

His eyes widen. "You know I do."

"Do you trust me?"

He hesitates.

"You should, because I've never given you a reason not to." He opens his mouth, but I gesture for him to stop. "For as long as I can remember, I've tried to please you." My heart hammers wildly as I think back, recalling those sleepless nights as a sad, lost little girl. "I was so scared you'd leave me and my brothers, just like Mom did."

He freezes, hardly breathing.

"You weren't around when we needed you. You worked, and we felt like we were second to that."

His brows furrow. "That was never…"

"No, Dad. It's my turn to talk and your turn to listen."

His mouth clamps shut, and for once, he doesn't argue.

I swallow down the nerves, knowing he needs to hear this. "I did everything I could to make you happy because I thought if I did, you'd be proud of me and give me your attention, give me more time with you… more time that I craved. I was always on my best behavior… I always got good grades. Even when you sent us away to private schools, I kept trying to be who I thought you wanted me to be."

His face falls. His eyes swirl with emotions, but I'm not so sure which ones.

"But it was never enough." I keep going, though ripping the stitches out of the wounds he caused hurts. "So, I started drinking alcohol, but you still never noticed how much I was drowning." I take a deep breath. "After school, I couldn't take it any longer, so I left." I chuckle, though it's flat. "I modeled to keep myself busy, but no matter how far I traveled, that pain stayed with me. Hell… I even started a business. I did it for myself, but that need for your approval… for you to be proud… is still ingrained in me…" *And I hate it… I hate it so much.*

"Your overprotectiveness to keep me safe is the only real love I've felt from you, so I've let you… all this time, I've let you be overbearing." I shake my head. "I understand why, but that stops now… Viper is my breaking point. I love him, Dad." My voice splinters at the end.

With a pale face, he stands and takes two steps toward me, but I take two steps back.

"You need to understand that I love you and your brothers," he says with conviction. Though my ears hear him, my heart struggles to believe him. This conversation with him is the first time he's said the words.

He shifts on his feet. "Working is all that I knew… it was what I was good at. Being a father… raising four kids…" He pauses, looking away, deep in thought. "I didn't know how, so I did what I thought was right by you and your brothers. I had others look after you… do what I didn't know how to do."

His words cut deep. My eyes burn, but I try to keep my composure.

"I was stern about your safety because I couldn't let what happened to your mother happen to you," he admits sadly. It's the haunted look in his eyes that makes the tears fall down my cheeks. "Being with Viper is dangerous… I can't…" —he shakes his head—"I can't have you in danger like that."

I stand tall. "But being with Viper makes me feel safe. He makes me feel loved, Dad." I stare at him, letting him see the pain in my eyes. "The only thing Viper loves is the club, and even when you threatened that, he still risked everything to be with me."

Dad's mouth pinches… he knows I'm right.

"I'm not Mom. I'm asking you to let go… I'm asking you to trust me…" I swallow. "I've chosen to be with Viper… if he still wants me, considering all the pain I've caused. And…"— my eyes narrow—"if you do anything that harms Viper… harms the club… the thing that you're afraid of will happen… you will lose me… forever."

Viper

. . .

IT'S TWO DAYS AFTER THE WEDDING. I'VE BEEN EXHAUSTING myself at the gym, and when I'm not there, I'm sitting at our bar in the clubhouse. I bring the beer to my lips and gulp some down. I feel shitty. I'm sure the alcohol isn't helping, but it eases the crushing feeling in my chest.

I faintly hear a squeal, then whispers, but I don't have it in me to turn around. *I'm tired... so very tired.* There's a tap on my shoulder, but I stay where I am. "Yes?" I grumble, not feeling like myself anymore.

There's a tap again, making me grind my teeth. I spin around to see Sophie's beautiful face, with those bright blue eyes. My breath quickens. "What are you doing here?" I ask. I thought we were going to spend time with each other before she went back to New York, but I never heard from her.

I stand, then notice a lot of luggage by her feet. "What's all this?" I ask. I force the excitement down. She could want me to take her to the airport.

She steps closer to me, then slowly loops her arms around my neck, and stands on her toes. Her piercing eyes study mine. "I'm here to stay married to you."

My smile grows until my cheeks hurt. I wrap my arms around her, pulling her in tight, nuzzling my head into her neck, then inch back. "What did your father have to say about it?"

"We had a good talk about everything. I told him how much he's hurt me and how much I love you and that if he doesn't honor my decision to be with you, he'll lose me. He knew I was serious, so he said he won't cause any more issues with you and the club."

I give her a chaste kiss on the lips. My heart could burst from happiness.

"But… I have a few provisions if I stay married to you," she says in a professional voice.

I laugh. "Of course you do. Well, go on… do tell me." I know I'd give her anything she wanted.

She clears her voice. "Just because I'll be living here doesn't mean I'm giving up my business. I'll be still working from home, but I'll be going back to New York once a month or when they need me."

Easy. "I can handle that. I respect your decision to run your business." I wouldn't let her give it up anyway. It makes her happy, and my life lights up when she smiles.

TWENTY-SEVEN
MC FAMILY

One Month Later

Sophie

All the ol' ladies and Milly are helping in the kitchen. I'm mixing up a salad to go with the barbecue for Ava's baby shower.

"Ahh!"

The shout makes me jump. I look at Ava, who's frozen, looking between her legs. I follow her line of sight to see Ava's pants wet in the crotch area.

Milly rushes to her side. "What's wrong?"

"I think my water just broke."

Milly peers down, then gives her a smile. "Yes, it looks like it has. Let's get you to the hospital."

. . .

Viper

Four hours later, the first MC baby made her way into the world. "What's the name again?" I ask Reaper, who holds his daughter in his arms, rocking from side to side. I feel bad for both the kid and Reaper. Second generation and the MC president's daughter—she's never going to have a dating life.

"Hope Elena White," Ava answers. Elena has the biggest smile on her face.

"Do you want to hold her?" asks Reaper, though the twitch at the corner of his mouth signifies he knows my answer.

"No, no, I'm all good." Sophie chuckles beside me.

"I will."

My head whips to Demon. Reaper's eyebrows are high on his forehead. He must be as shocked as I am. Demon moves to Reaper, who gently passes the baby in the pink blanket to Demon's arms. The pure smile on Demon's face surprises me. His tattoos are such a contrast against the simple pink blanket and pale arms and face of the newborn.

The room is quiet, but there's a collective sigh from the women. I can see them all melt as we gaze at Hope. Axle's laugh breaks the silence. "You're the last person I ever thought would hold the baby."

Demon gazes lovingly at Hope before he peers up at Axle. "I love kids. It's the adults I don't like."

After making sure Ava and bub are okay, we give Ava and Reaper time to bond with their baby girl.

Sophie

• • •

WHEN AVA RETURNS TO THE CLUBHOUSE THE NEXT DAY, WE reorganize the food and festivities to celebrate Hope's birth. I pop upstairs to grab the present I got for the baby, then return to see Cash placing the meat in the middle of the table outside. Everyone takes their seats. I step over to Ava with an outstretched arm.

Her eyes widen when they latch onto what I'm holding. "Another present? You've already spent too much," says Ava.

All the MC put in money to get the baby a stroller and baby furniture, but I had this planned for a long time. "I had already ordered this. It just took some time to come in the mail."

Ava gently takes the small present from me. "Thank you," she replies and starts unwrapping it. She pulls out a white onesie and looks at the front of it. She laughs and then turns it around, raising it in the air so everyone can see. It has a stamp —a vest with the War Brothers MC patch logo at the back.

"It's so cute," she says in a high-pitched voice.

I smile back and go to take a seat, but the chair beside mine where Viper usually sits is empty. I gaze around the backyard, but I can't see him. The bang of the back door closing makes me turn. It's Viper with his usual infectious smile and a leather vest in his hands.

He's so goddamn sexy. He makes his way to me, lifting up a leather vest. Excitement shoots through me. "Is this for me?" I say through a smile.

"Yes, it is, wifey."

I place my arms in the holes and bring the vest up. The leather is heavier than I remember. I glance down to see the "Property of Viper" patch. "Thank you," I say to him. He leans down, grabs my chin, and pulls me in for a long, sweet kiss, which I eagerly return. Everyone claps around us.

I peer at Cash. "Mr. Tall, Dark, and Handsome, you've finally come through with the goods." He chuckles at me.

Viper takes a seat and pulls me onto his lap, making me squeal in surprise. "I'm so happy you came back to me. My favorite place in the world is by your side, and life just isn't as colorful without you in it."

By popular demand, **Axle and Elena's** story is coming soon. Pre-order is $0.99.

Get ready for **Twitch and Milly's** story… or will it be **Demon and Ivy, Cash and Sienna,** or **Rage and Rose?** Sign up for my mailing list to be the first to hear about it.

RESOURCES

One Australian dollar of every paperback book purchase from Bianca's website will go to the LifeLine charity.

If you are struggling with your mental health, contact LifeLine. LifeLine is available in many countries and offers help for people experiencing emotional distress. They provide confidential crisis support, and in most instances, you can call, chat online, or text.

Please visit https://lifeline-intl.com/our-network/ for more information.

If you are seeking help with a drinking problem, contact Alcoholics Anonymous. AA is an informal society that operates in many countries and offers peer support for recovery from alcoholism.

Please visit https://www.aa.org/find-aa/world for more information.

ACKNOWLEDGMENTS

This is short and sweet. Special thanks to Silvia and the Proofreading Services team for their editing, my mom Carol for her unwavering support, and to all my readers - your support and patience mean the world to me.

Stay tuned for more,

Bianca Lee Ward

ABOUT THE AUTHOR

Bianca Lee Ward is an Australian romance author with a love of culinary adventures and a playlist for every mood. She enjoys exploring themes of identity, personal growth, and resilience in her work—with a little spice on the side. When she isn't lost in storytelling or absorbed in her latest read, Bianca can be found watching true crime stories and documentaries.

You can connect with Bianca online at:
Website: www.biancaleeward.com
Email: info@biancaleeward.com
Instagram: https://www.instagram.com/biancaleeward
Facebook: https://www.facebook.com/biancaleeward
Spotify: Bianca Lee Ward
Pinterest: https://www.pinterest.com.au/biancaleeward
Goodreads: https://www.goodreads.com/author/show/30477361.Bianca_Lee_Ward
BookBub: https://www.bookbub.com/authors/bianca-lee-ward

Don't forget to sign up to Bianca's mailing list, where you'll get *huge* discounts, *exclusive* giveaways, and new release alerts!